UNBOUND

SUTTON SNOW
TINLEY BLAKE

Printed in the United States of America

First Printing, 2019

www.tinleyblake.com

content warning

THIS E-BOOK CONTAINS SEXUALLY explicit scenes and adult language, and may be considered offensive to some readers. The characters in this book are cynical, hard to love, and horny. This is a forbidden romance, age gap, slightly taboo story filled with smut. It is intended for sale to adults only, as defined by the laws of the country in which you made your purchase. Please store your files wisely where they cannot be accessed by under-aged readers.

Theme song

Hell on Heels by Pistol Annies

dedication

For all the women who have found their Happily
Ever After and all the ones still looking.
Don't worry, Girl. He's there.
He just might be dating your best friend.

(Kidding)

prologue

Harriet

I TOSS my keys on the table as I shut the door behind me, heaving a sigh of relief. My latest client couldn't decide on a clothing choice, so I ended up shooting her in five different outfits. What should have taken an hour and a half at the most ended up being almost four hours long. Some days, it's easy to forget that I love what I do.

Pulling my phone from my pocket, I unlock it but stop before checking my messages when I hear soft sobs coming from the living room.

Shit.

I barely manage to hold in the groan of frustration. I know exactly who it is without seeing her face. She sent over ten messages in the past hour, each more dramatic than the last. It's not Kennady's fault I had a long day, but damn, I really wanted a hot bath and glass . . . no, an entire bottle of wine.

"Kennady? What's wrong?" I ask, rounding the corner.

She lifts her head, tears streaming down her puffy face. "How can you ask me that? You know what's wrong."

Stepping fully into the living room, I grab a box of tissues and pull a few free, passing them to her. "He left me," she says, hiccupping. "No, that's a lie. He didn't even have the decency to break up with me. He just started dating someone else."

I sit on the couch next to her, rubbing gentle circles across her back. "Are you talking about the guy you met last week? I didn't know you guys were together." I try to be the voice of reason as gently as I can, but the truth is that my best friend has a habit of falling fast and hard, then being crushed when it doesn't work out. This is the second guy this month I have found her in tears over, and something tells me it won't be the last.

"Of course we were. I mean, we didn't discuss

exactly what we were to each other, but that only happens in movies and books."

I nod my head without speaking. At this point in the conversation, she doesn't want my words. She just needs to be heard and to get it all out.

"I was with him Wednesday, and then today he was out with a random girl hanging on his arm. I tried to message him, but . . ." She trails off, and I know without looking that she probably overreacted and went full-on psycho.

"Let me see."

She passes her phone to me, and I scroll through their text exchange all the way to the top. Eight days. She met him eight days ago. Scrolling back to the bottom, I locate the beginning of their messages for today. He genuinely sounds surprised that she would find an issue with him dating. According to the messages, he'd told her repeatedly that he wasn't looking for anything long-term. She even agreed that they would just have fun and see where it went. Of course, I know her sly *see where it goes* comment was more than just acceptance of his terms. Kennady wouldn't know how to only have fun with a man. She is a true believer in soulmates. Unfortunately, she believes every man who shows her the least bit of attention is fated to be hers.

Passing her phone back to her, I rack my brain for something to say. Thankfully, she fills the silence for me. "I just wish he knew how this felt. It's not okay to string someone along and then cut them loose without even a word."

"I know it hurts, baby girl. But if that's the man he is, then he doesn't deserve you anyway."

"You're probably right, but I really thought we had something special. I feel so stupid now."

"You're not stupid. You just trust too easily, and you wear your heart on your sleeve."

She nods her head, sniffling. "I wish I were more like you. You don't let anyone close enough to hurt you."

I try not to let the comment sting. Try and fail. It's not that I don't want love, but life has taught me that there is no such thing as a happily ever after. Maybe one day, I'll find someone who can at least offer me a happy for now. But so far, no one has been willing to scale the wall built around my heart.

"How about a glass of wine? That always manages to cheer me up."

Kennady nods, and I stand, walking into the kitchen. I fill two glasses with chilled Moscato and carry them back to the living room. Kennady's tears have dried up, her eyes now narrowed on the screen of her phone. I glance over her shoulder to see she has his Instagram pulled up.

"Girl, stop. Don't waste another second thinking of him. He's not worth it."

"It's so hard," she says, taking the offered glass from my hand. "Maybe if I knew he was hurting too, it would make me feel better."

"You don't mean that. You hate when others are in pain."

"Okay, maybe not hurting, but someone really does need to give him a taste of his own medicine."

"I'm sure someone will one day. And then he will realize how he made all the women before feel."

"Exactly," she says, taking a sip. I lift my glass and let the sweet tang of wine wash the day away.

"Harriet!"

I nearly choke on the swallow, coughing to make sure it doesn't go down the wrong pipe.

"You should do it."

"Do what?" I ask, dumbfounded.

"Give him a taste of his own medicine."

Shaking my head, I open my mouth to say no. "Kenn . . ."

"No. Hear me out. You don't get attached. Hell, most of the time, you barely give men the time of day, so I know you won't get pulled in by

SUTTON SNOW & TINLEY BLAKE

his charm. I know it's asking a lot, but please do this for me."

"I . . . I can't do that. I don't even know this man. How would I even find him? And what then?"

"Finding him is easy. I know all his favorite places. I compiled a list of his tagged locations when we started dating. You just need to show up, looking like a knockout, and he will approach you."

Of course she did. I open my mouth to tell her that sort of thing isn't normal but stop. Nothing I say will make her see the truth. "And then what?" I ask, even though I really don't want to know. This is the most insane thing I've ever heard of.

"Go out with him. Sleep with him, and then kick him to the curb. Make him wonder what he did wrong, why you're ignoring him. Make him feel the way he made me feel."

"You want me to revenge fuck a man for you?"

"Yes! It's perfect. He'll never see it coming."

"And then I ignore him. That's it. One date and done."

"That's it. Please, Harriet, do this for me, and I promise I'll never ask another thing of you as long as I live."

"Pinky swear?"

She lifts her hand, offering her pinkie. I lock mine around it and touch my thumb to hers. "Pinky swear."

This has to be the stupidest, most idiotic thing I have ever agreed to in my life.

The thought has been circling my mind for the last hour, ever since I meticulously applied my makeup and took the curlers out of my hair, letting it fall in soft waves down my back.

I should be home in the bed, binging Gilmore Girls, not shivering in a way too short to be considered modest dress while I wait for the bouncer to check my ID. Instead, I'm about to do the most insane thing ever attempted. *You got this, Hare. Catch his eye, and then let the games begin.*

I spent the evening draining a bottle of wine and scrolling Pacey McIntyre's social media so I could recognize him when I saw him. Not that it was needed. I don't think I would ever get the image of those striking green eyes out of my head anytime soon. He's a photographer's holy grail of subjects, and I would literally kill to see him behind the lens.

After a long glance and a grunt of approval, the

bouncer ushers me inside. The place is low-lit but still bright enough to see across the room. I slowly make my way across the floor and lean against the bar. My eyes rake over the bar and then the tables that are scattered around. I spot a group of guys on the far end and who I think may be Pacey, but I can't be sure unless he comes closer.

Luckily, or unluckily, depending on how you look at it, he raises his head, scanning the bar, and his eyes lock on mine. I lift one side of my mouth in a half grin and turn to face the barkeep, breaking eye contact. Even facing away from him, I can still feel his eyes on me, traveling the length of my bare legs.

"What can I get you?"

"Gin and tonic, please."

He nods and starts preparing the drink. Fighting the urge to glance back at the table of guys, I dig into my clutch, pulling out my debit card. The cool glass slides along the bar, the ice settling.

"Five fifty."

Raising my arm to pass over my card, I'm surprised when a hand covers my own. "Put it on my tab, Rick."

Glancing up, my gaze meets clear green eyes. I

bite my tongue to keep from arguing and smile my thanks.

"It's only fair," he says, releasing my hand. Damn, he really is good-looking. Tall, a chiseled jawline, dark hair, and a smile that would knock the panties off any woman. That last thought drags me out from under the spell of his charm. Not only is he capable of getting any woman he wants, but he does. Quite frequently, if Kennady is to be believed.

"What's that? I ask.

"That I buy your drink. After all, it's not every day an angel walks the earth."

I laugh at the ridiculousness. "Does that line ever work?"

He shrugs, grinning. "Not my best work. How about you grab that drink, and I'll try out a few more? Maybe a different one is more to your liking."

I consider how to play this. Regardless, I'm going to follow him, but he doesn't know that. His grin starts to slip, and I know I need to speak quickly before he loses all interest. "On one condition."

"Okay, let's have it."

Reaching for the drink, I pull it to me and take

a small sip. "You only get three chances. After that, you're out."

His eyes light up, and the grin is replaced with a full-fledged smile. My heart trips in my chest, sputtering. "Three strikes and you're out? Deal. But I should warn you, I never strike out."

This time, when I reply, my own smile is bright. Dazzling. "I'm counting on it." Placing my hand on his arm, I let him lead from the bar to a table on the opposite side from his friends. I don't bother asking why we didn't go there.

Two hours and three drinks later, I'm feeling every bit of Gin. If I hadn't walked into this place fully prepared to take him home with me, I would still be considering it. He's everything I usually look for in a man—funny, smart, and damn good-looking.

And not available.

We take his car back to my place, and after fumbling with the keys for longer than I'd like to admit, we're inside. The door closes behind me, and then his hands are on my waist, his lips pressed to mine.

My back presses against the wall, my hands digging into his shirt, lifting it. He breaks the kiss for a moment and lets me tug it over his head, then his mouth is back on mine. Every touch of his tongue sends shivers of awareness through my body.

My clothes are left discarded in small piles, making a trail through the house to my bedroom. Every place his hands touch comes alive until my body is trembling like a live wire. My legs hit the bed, and I fall backward, pulling him with me, never breaking the kiss.

Pacey's fingers trail up the inside of my thighs, searching, seeking. My legs fall open, giving him easy access, my body craving his touch. His fingers slip through the wetness there, teasing. I moan in the back of my throat when he doesn't give me what I so desperately seek.

"Easy, Kitten. I promise before this is over, I will make your body purr. Now spread those legs for me and let me feast on that pretty pussy."

Fucking hell. I've never been big on dirty talk in the bedroom, but something about the way he says it doesn't sound cringy. My legs widen farther for him, and he wastes no time sliding down my body and nestling between my thighs.

"Mmm, look at that bare pussy. She's practically pulsing with need," he says, leaning forward and placing a soft kiss on my clit. My hips lift, begging for more.

His tongue darts out, flicking across the

bundle of nerves. My hands tangle in his hair, pressing his face closer to me. He chuckles, pulling away. Taking my hands in each of his, he presses them to the sides of my body. "Don't move. Don't make a sound. If you do . . . well, Kitten, you wouldn't like that."

I try to pull away, try to open my mouth and ask who the hell he thinks he is, but then his tongue is licking up the seam of my pussy, his lips wrapping around the hood of my clit and his mouth suckling me into the hot haven. Every complaint dies on my tongue. Holy fucking hell.

A whimper of need breaks through my parted lips, and he stops. His eyes meet mine, and in them, I read the challenge. Understanding washes over me. If I follow his rules, he will give me what I want . . . what I need. If not, he will leave me wanting. Pulling my bottom lip between my teeth, I bite down and offer what I hope is an apologetic look.

Satisfied that I understand, he leans down and flicks his tongue across me again, never taking his eyes off mine. My hands grip the sheets, twisting, but I don't reach for him. I don't open my mouth and beg him for more.

The room is silent except for the sound of his mouth on me. I give myself over to that sound, my mind acutely focused on every pass of his tongue through me, every brush of his five-o'clock shadow across the inside of my thigh. My orgasm is building, cresting, and threatening to swallow me whole.

"Now, come for me," he says, pushing a finger inside.

I shatter around him, my body quivering, pulsing with each wave of ecstasy. His tongue slows, the flicks easing into gentle laps against my sensitive clit. I could stay here forever in this post-orgasmic bliss, but he clearly has other plans. A second finger joins the first, pumping into me with agonizing slowness, stretching me . . . filling me.

"Good girl. Now do it again."

I almost groan, almost open my mouth and tell him there is no way I'll be able to come again this soon, but then he pulls his fingers out and runs them through the slick wetness between my thighs before pushing back inside me.

Fuck.

The sounds of my pussy sucking his fingers deep into me and his palm slapping against my clit have my body reaching once more. I block out the disbelief, pushing any and all doubt from my mind. Never mind that no other man has made me have multiple orgasms. This man clearly knows what he's doing.

Just when I feel the first tremors of release, he stills. I fight the urge to grind my hips against his hand. "Not yet, Kitten. I want to feel you come on my cock."

Easing to his knees, he takes his cock in his hand and strokes up and down the length of it. My eyes widen when I see the silver of barbells glistening in the light. Up the backside of his cock, there are five—no, six—barbells piercing his skin.

"You think this pretty pussy is ready for me now?" he asks, rubbing his cock down my slit and back up again before slapping its head against my clit. I raise my legs, wrapping them around his waist rather than replying.

His only reply is sliding deep inside me, burying every inch of his sizable length in my wet heat. His hands grip my hips, lifting my ass while pulling my body closer, and then he slides out and slams home once again.

"Does that feel good, baby?"

My back arches, my eyes closed tightly. Goosebumps light across my skin, up my arms, down my legs. One hand releases my hip, only to reappear at the apex of my thighs, circling and teasing my clit in gentle circles.

"Tell me how good it feels, Kitten. Do you want me to make you come?"

"*Yessss.*"

He chuckles before driving into me with renewed vigor. The storm is building, cresting, reaching higher and higher with each stroke of his cock. My arms lift, my hands gripping his thighs, my fingers digging into the flesh there.

Stars erupt across my vision when I shatter. He pumps into me once, twice, and then he growls low in his throat as his own orgasm chases mine. Hot seed fills me, coating the walls of my pussy, dripping down the crack of my ass with each pump of his cock. I ride the wave through every break, rising and falling until he slips from me and runs a hand through the mess between my thighs.

"Fuck, you're beautiful with my cum coating your thighs. I could stay here forever."

Slowly, the fog of release fades, and with it, a memory snakes back in. I'm not supposed to enjoy this. I have one simple job to do. Scooting up the bed, I slide my legs over the side and stand on wobbly legs. How the hell did I forget the plan? Fuck him and then destroy him. That's it.

Grabbing a semi-clean towel off the back of my reading chair, I toss it to him and head to the bathroom. His cum is still slick between my legs, dripping with each step I take. When I reach the door, I look over my shoulder and grin. "You remember where the door is, right? Don't be here when I come back out."

Stepping into the bathroom, I shut the door and lean against the counter, listening intently for sounds of him gathering his things. When I hear the front door click shut, I turn on the shower and wait for steam to fill the room. Fucking hell. How did I let the night get away from me?

Fortunately, I can no longer see my reflection in the mirror. Stepping into the shower, I do my best to wash away every trace of Pacey McIntyre, but with each pass of my hands, images and sounds flood my mind.

What the hell have I gotten myself into?

present
day

Pacey

chapter one

LEANING my head against the wall, I try to block out the raging music blasting through the bar. People come here to eat. They could at least keep the volume down until after dinner.

Lifting my phone, I check it for the hundredth time in the last ten minutes, but there are no new messages. I don't know how to do this shit. I'm not a whiny bitch who falls for someone after the first hookup. I'm the guy who walks away.

I don't do relationships. Never have and never will.

So why the fuck is this chick getting to me?

We had a good time. At least, I thought we did. And then when we finished, she stood up, grabbed a towel, and tossed my clothes to me with a dry

"You remember where the door is, right? Don't be here when I come back out."

I was too stunned to do anything other than get dressed and leave.

It's been three fucking weeks, and I haven't heard a peep from her. Today, I finally got up the nerve to call her, but it went straight to voicemail, so I followed it up with a text inviting her out tonight.

Glancing at my phone again, I open Messages. *Nothing. Zilch. Nada.* Closing out of that app, I text Ash just to make sure the fucking thing works.

"Dude, did you just text me WYD? You know I'm sitting right here next to you."

"Fuck off. I know that. I was just checking my phone."

"Aw, leave him alone, Ash. You know he doesn't know what to do with all these feelings," Lucy says, striding up to the table. It's her twenty-first birthday, and when Weston asked her what she wanted to do, this is what she came up with.

All of us here, at the bar where she first met Weston. Her eyes light up with mirth, and if I weren't in such a shitty mood, I'd pick back at her. But this chick has me all out of sorts. I don't know what's up from down or left from right anymore.

It's fucking pathetic.

"Harriet still hasn't reached out?" Lucy asks, her gaze narrowing on the phone clutched in my hand.

"Not a fucking word," I grunt out.

"Maybe she died," Weston offers, joining the conversation.

"She didn't fucking die, you sick fuck." The words are barked out.

He shrugs, turning up his beer. "She could have. I mean, what other woman would ignore you this long? You tried to call her?" he asks.

"Yes. And I messaged her. But I know she isn't dead. She posted to social media yesterday," I say, twirling my bottle on the table.

"Jesus, Pace, you're cyberstalking her?" Lucy gasps, shocked.

"No. Yes? Fuck, I don't know what I'm doing." Placing my head in my hands, I rub my forehead. When did my life get so twisted?

The guys all laugh at my expense, but Lucy's eyes fill with sympathy. And isn't that just fucking great.

"I know how to make her stop ignoring you, but you might not like it," she offers, her tone edged with a wicked delight.

I practically leap in my seat at the chance. "How? Tell me."

"Hand me your phone," she says before standing on her tiptoes and whispering something in Weston's ear. He grins and nods.

Eyeing her warily, I pass her my phone. She opens the camera app and checks her reflection on the screen. After adjusting her top to show way more cleavage than I need to see, she slides between my legs, her back pressed against my chest, and holds the camera high.

"Smile or nuzzle my hair and pretend like you're having the time of your life."

"What?" I ask, almost positive I heard her wrong, but she just stares at me, waiting.

"Just do it."

I follow her direction and try not to flinch when she turns her face toward mine and presses her lips to my cheek. She snaps a few pics and then mercifully steps away. Glancing at Weston, I brace myself, but he just smiles and slaps my shoulder.

After a few minutes, Lucy passes my phone back, a wicked grin gracing her face. "If she doesn't text within ten minutes, write her off. But I'd bet my left tit that she is stalking you as much as you are her and she will—"

She doesn't even get the chance to finish the sentence before my phone vibrates on the counter. I stare in wonder as Harriet's name flashes across the top. I reach for it, but Lucy lays a hand on top of mine, stopping me.

"Not yet. Let her sweat it out," she says, grinning.

"What the hell did you do?" I can't fucking believe it. Less than a minute. That's all it took.

"It's the oldest trick in the book. I just made her think you had moved on." Opening her own phone, she pulls up my Instagram, and right there for the world to see is Lucy in my arms with the caption, *backed by your number one* with two heart emoticons.

Damn. I shake my head. Picking up my phone, I slip it into my back pocket and take a swig of my beer. So far, everything Lucy has done has worked, so if she says to let her sweat it out, then I'll leave her in a puddle.

Not how I wanted her attention, but I can't deny there is a sick satisfaction to be had knowing she was stalking me as much as I was her. I knew it. Now I just need to figure out how to play this, and more importantly, why we're playing a game at all.

One thing is for certain. Regardless of the whos, whats, and whys, I will win this game. And when I have her, she'll wish she'd never started playing at all.

harriet

chapter Two

TUCKING my phone back into my pocket, I try to hide the creeping blush spreading up my neck. I've never been a shy person, but the moment I try to lie, my face will give it all away. My mom used to say it was a built-in lie detector, not that I spent much time lying to her anyway. She was and is one of my favorite people in the world.

"So, do you want to go?" Kennady asks.

"When is it again?"

"Tomorrow. We'll make a weekend of it and come back Sunday night."

"Oh, damn. I can't. I have a client," I say, standing so she can't see my face. There's no way I can tell her the real reason I can't go is because I just agreed to another date with Pacey. As far as she knows, it was just a onetime thing and I left him wondering what the hell went wrong. Most of that is true. What she doesn't know is he has texted me a handful of times each week since that night and even tried to call me once. I should have blocked his number, should have erased him from my mind and pretended nothing ever happened.

The truth is that I haven't been able to stop thinking about him. And not just the mind-blowing, earth-shattering sex, but everything that came before that too. We spent hours talking at the bar, and not once was there a lull in the conversation. He spoke of his work without being braggy and then showed real interest in what I do for a living. He even pulled me up on his phone and started looking through some of my work online, asking questions about inspiration and how I managed to secure a certain shot.

In short, I really enjoyed it. If I had met him any other way, I would have responded to the first text and jumped at the opportunity to go on another date.

"Oh my God, Harriet. Look at this." I turn in time to see Kennady shove her phone in my face. "I guess I should have known he wouldn't be affected by you. And he posted her? He's never posted a girl. Ever. I scrolled to the beginning of his feed and checked."

I shrug my shoulders, letting her comments roll off. "Oh, well. He looks happy."

"We don't want him happy. We want him miserable and pining after someone he can't have."

"I tried, Kennady. What do you want me to do?"

"Maybe you should try again." She tilts her head toward the ceiling like she's thinking about it. "Yeah. I should have known one date with you wouldn't be enough. I think you should run into him again."

"Why? You've moved on. You say you're happy with Chuck, right? So what does it matter?"

"I am happy, but that doesn't mean I want him to be."

"That makes no sense. Just let the man live his life."

"Whatever. You probably wouldn't be able to pull it off, anyway. It's no wonder he's already moved on. I should have known you weren't up for it."

I shake my head. "And what if I did, Ken? What if I went back out with him and things went great? Huh? What if it ended up being more than just some twisted game you created?"

She throws back her head, laughing. "Like love? You think you can make him fall in love with you? Oh, Harriet, you don't know the first thing about love."

"Wow. You're right. I guess I don't. Or maybe I just don't know about your shallow misinterpretation of the act."

"What's that supposed to mean?" she asks.

"Nothing. Don't worry about it."

Walking back into the living room, I grab my purse and keys. Chuck still sits on the couch, showing no reaction to the conversation going on in the kitchen five feet away. Kennady steps to his side, running her fingers through his hair. Her gaze meets mine, hard and unforgiving. I don't bother saying goodbye before pulling the door shut behind me.

I try to push the argument with her to the back of my mind. But this time, I can't seem to shake her words. How dare she insinuate that I'm incapable of being loved. It's not like she hasn't said things like this before, but I usually brush them off, assuming she doesn't realize she's being cruel. Tonight was different. She knew exactly what she was doing. I could see the calculation in her eyes before she attacked.

A small part of me wonders if she's right. I've never been in love, never let a man get close enough for that. I'm not even sure I would want to. Love seems like the biggest mistake most people make in life. Giving yourself over to someone so completely that they hold the power to break you? No, thank you.

Now having fun, enjoying a mutually beneficial give-and-take relationship? That I can do.

Grinning, I pull my phone from my pocket and text Pacey. Fun. I can do this. I deserve it, right? I hit *Send* and stop on the corner, waiting for the light to change, and watch the three bubbles appear at the bottom.

Pacey: What do you have in mind?

Me: Just some fun.

Pacey: I can do that.

Me: My place or yours?

Pacey: Mine. I plan to tie you to the bed so you can't run off this time.

I stumble, nearly walking into a bench when I read the line. Of course, he wouldn't have forgotten the way I kicked him out last time.

Me: Promises, promises.

Me: Send me the address.

When it comes through, I copy and paste it into Maps to see if it's within walking distance, then sigh and open the Uber app. Once I've scheduled the drive, I sit on the bench that almost took me out and wait for my ride to pull up. The night air is brisk, but the sky is clear. This is my favorite time of year, when the days are mildly warm and the nights start cooling off. I love to walk the city with nothing but the moon for company.

Me: See you in thirty.

Pacey

chapter three

I'D JUST WALKED through the door when my phone dinged. Expecting a text from Ash or Weston, I almost dropped my phone when I saw Harriet's name pop up.

Rushing through the house, I make sure there aren't any dirty clothes lying around and then spend five minutes making my bed. Never in a million years did I expect Lucy's plan to work out so well.

Weeks. That's how long I've been trying to get in touch with this woman, and within minutes of posting that photo, she texted. And now she's on her way here. It could be a coincidence. Maybe she didn't even see the picture and just decided to reach out. She could have seen the missed call and . . .

No matter how I spin it in my head, it doesn't

make sense. She had to have seen it. The question is why would seeing me with another woman make her want to contact me? If she wanted to ensure I was available, she could have done that with a text back anytime. It's almost like seeing me with someone else made her jealous.

I grin, imagining her reaction. I would pay good money to have seen the look on her face when she was scrolling. And now she's on her way here. I don't normally bring women back here. It makes it too hard to get them to leave the next day. Not to mention, the ones who show up randomly, uninvited, and then make a scene when I ask them to leave.

Somehow, I don't think I have to worry about that with Harriet. She didn't strike me as the clingy type. And judging by how she ended the last date, I don't think getting her to leave will be a problem. Now talking her into staying . . .

The chime of the doorbell rings through the house, and I fight the urge to race to the door. Never in my life have I been so anxious and excited about a woman showing up. Pulling open the door, I lean back and gesture for her to enter.

She looks fucking irresistible in skin-tight jeans that hug every curve. The loose sweater hits just above her waist, and with every movement, a small

UNBOUND

piece of flesh peeks out. I want nothing more than to drop to my knees and run my tongue along that spot.

"Come in. Can I get you something to drink?" I ask, shutting the door behind her.

She stops just inside the entryway, her eyes darting across the space. Placing my hand on her lower back, I lead her toward the center of the house. Stopping by a sideboard, I grab a couple of glasses and pour two fingers of bourbon into each. She takes the glass when offered and lifts it to her nose, inhaling the sweet, mellow aroma.

Glasses in hand, I lead her upstairs. She seems different tonight. Glancing at her from the side, I watch as her eyes take in everything around her, but her mind is somewhere else. Even though she texted me for some fun tonight, I have a feeling she is readying herself, and that just won't do.

Making a spontaneous decision, I stop and lean down to whisper in her ear. "What you're about to see is one of my deepest, darkest secrets. Not many know about it, and those who do have promised to never share details."

Her eyes widen a fraction. I grin at the reaction.

"Can I trust you?"

Her gaze meets mine, warm honey eyes holding

mine for a moment before she nods. She looks terrified and intrigued all rolled into one, but the haunted look in her eyes has faded for now. Reaching up, I tuck a stray strand of blonde hair behind her ear. "Brace yourself."

Twisting the knob, I push open the door and step inside. Harriet follows slowly. I reach beside the door and flick on a switch, illuminating the room. Her breath rushes out in a soft gasp.

"Books!" Her hand slaps my chest. "I thought you were leading me to a secret red room or something. My heart almost leapt from my chest!"

Grinning, I walk across the room and sit on one of the soft plush couches in the center of the room. Harriet spins in circles, her eyes taking it all in before darting to the shelf closest to her. Her fingers lift, lovingly tracing the spine of a book before moving to another shelf across the room.

I watch her flit around, savoring each gasp and low moan of appreciation. After a few minutes, she joins me on the couch. "How long have you been collecting them?" she asks.

"Most of my life." I shrug. "When I was young, reading offered an escape from the real world and my life. As I got older, it became my release, in a way. My therapy."

Her head nods as if she understands. "What is your favorite?"

I laugh at the idea. "I couldn't pick if I had to."

"Yeah, I can understand that. You have so many, it would be hard to choose."

"Do you have a favorite?"

She shakes her head, eyeing the shelves around her. "I can't choose either."

Her smile is so wistful, so full of longing and love, I can't help but lean over and press my mouth to hers. Her lips are as soft as sin and smell like freshly baked apple pie. Her hand lifts, running down my bicep gently, pulling me closer. When her mouth opens, my tongue darts forth, tangling with her own.

Our breath mingles with each inhale and exhale, the act intoxicatingly erotic. I shift on the couch, my cock rubbing against my jeans. The urge to strip her naked right here and devour her consumes me, but she isn't getting off that easily. Running my hands up her thighs I press against the heat between her legs. She's beyond ready, but this isn't going to be easy for her. Not after the last time. Not after she fucked me with that glorious body of hers and then kicked me out without so much as a thank you. No. She's going to work for this orgasm. Starting with doing exactly as I say.

Breaking away from her delectable mouth, I stand, putting space between us. "My bedroom is two doors down on the right. Go there now. Strip, get on your knees, and wait for me."

"What?"

Stepping closer, I pull a piece of hair between my fingers and tug. Leaning forward, I whisper in her ear, "I'm going to fuck you, Kitten. I'm going to make your body purr for me, but only if you do exactly as I say."

She steps back, her eyes wide. I hold her gaze, quirking a single brow in question. That seems to spur her into motion, whatever questions and doubts she had floating away. Turning, she races from the room.

Reaching down, I adjust my cock in my jeans, grab my forgotten glass of bourbon, and swallow it in one gulp. Already, my mind is filling with thoughts on what I can do to her . . . for her. After about five minutes, I leisurely walk from the room and head down the hall.

Harriet is buck ass naked on my bed, sideways. All I see is the glistening slit of her pussy when I walk in. My cock throbs in my jeans, begging to plant itself inside her and lose myself.

Not yet.

I ignore her questioning gaze as I pass the bed

and start stripping my clothes off, making sure to hold her gaze the entire time. My cock bobs with each step closer to her, the silver jewelry glistening in the low light. Curling my fingers in her hair, I pull her head closer. "Wrap those pretty lips around my cock, Kitten, and suck like your life depends on it."

harriet

chapter four

LEANING FORWARD, I open my mouth, wrapping my lips around the head of his cock. My tongue darts out, running along the ridge around his head. My pussy clenches at the thought of him filling me, of that swollen head pressing inside me, sliding deeper and deeper.

I moan deep in my throat, my hips flexing and rolling, trying desperately to relieve some of the unbearable need. Lifting a hand, I wrap it around the base of Pacey's cock and slide my mouth down his length. I can't physically fit more than half in my mouth, and not just because it is at least eight inches long. No, the damn thing is so thick that opening my mouth wide enough while still taking him into my throat is next to impossible.

The silver barbells piercing the underside rub across my lips, the feeling foreign and exciting.

Once I've taken as much of him as possible, I slide my hand up to meet my lips and pull back. His hips flex, his hand tight in my hair, but I don't stop working him over. "Stop," he says, taking a step back. I release his dick with a pop of my lips and glance up at him.

"Lie back on the bed and raise your arms above your head."

There's a little voice in my head screaming to tell him to go fuck himself. No man tells me what to do and how to do it. Unfortunately, there is a much louder voice demanding that I listen to every word he says. I never thought I'd be one of those girls who likes to be dominated, but he makes it so fucking erotic that I can't argue.

Leaning back on his pillows, I do as he says and stretch my arms above my head. His answering grin sends zings of electricity straight to my core. My gaze follows him as he steps closer to the bed and reaches around the headboard. When I see the strap, that little voice breaks through. "What are you doing?"

"You didn't think I was joking with you, did you? I told you I was going to make sure you couldn't escape this time."

"But—"

"Don't worry, Kitten. I'll let you out eventually, but not until I finish imprinting the feel of my cock on your womb."

Holy fuck buckets. Who says shit like that? Damn sure, not any of the men I've been with. But to be honest, if they had, I probably would have left the room laughing. It takes a certain confidence to pull that kind of shit, and let me just say that Pacey has confidence in spades.

I pass him my wrist, wondering if I have possibly lost my ever-loving mind. A few hours ago, I was dead-set on never seeing this man again. Then he posted that picture, and my gut twisted at the thought of him with her. I have no right. For all I know, that woman is his girlfriend and I am the adulterous whore. The thought sours my stomach.

"Do you think this is a good idea? What if someone shows up here? How will I get out?"

"No one comes here uninvited."

"Your girlfriend doesn't have a key?"

"I don't have a girlfriend."

"Oh. What about the woman you posted?"

Yes, I know I just gave myself away, but what choice did I have? I need to know before we take this any further. He smirks, lifting my other arm. "You don't have to worry about her."

"Who—" the question is cut off when he runs

a hand down my chest, his fingers pinching my pebbled nipple between their tips.

"There is only one woman I'm worried about right now, and she is currently tied to my bed. Now do you want to discuss other women, or do you want to close those perfect lips and let me worship this pussy?"

I snap my mouth shut. Sure, there is a lot I'd like to say, but the memory of his mouth on my pussy keeps me from doing so. I've dreamt of nothing but his head between my legs for weeks now, successfully berating myself every day for not returning his calls. But I'm not in this for a relationship. I want the sex. The fun. And God knows, he can give me that.

He watches me like he expects more snappy comments, but the closer his head gets to my pussy, the less I can think. Warm breath tickles my skin, and then his mouth descends.

Holy saints. No playback or memory could ever compete with the way his mouth feels on me. Just when I think I have literally died and gone to heaven, he stops and trails kisses up my body. I'm on fire. My skin melts at his touch. Then he pulls another piece of cloth out and lays it over my eyes. With deft fingers, it's secured, and suddenly, I'm tossed into a chasm of darkness.

My heart beats rapidly in my chest, racing to escape whatever he has planned. Slowly, the sound of my pulse in my ears recedes, and I can hear more noises. A zipper. Some cloth. With my eyesight blocked, every other sense kicks into overdrive.

Something soft tickles my breast. I try to pull my arm down to swat it away, but I can't move. I can't do anything but lie here as he tortures my body and mind.

The tickling soft sensation leaves my breast and trails down my stomach, across my thigh, and gently flutters against my clit. My legs drop open wider.

I moan low in my throat when I feel his breath against me there again. Teeth graze against me, and my hips flex, running from or leaning into the sensation, I don't know.

I have never in my life been so out of control of a situation, and I don't know how I feel about it. A part of me is relishing in this freedom, letting him do whatever he wants to me. But another part is freaking out. I am the one in control. I refuse to give anyone power over me, even physically. It's terrifying. And exhilarating.

I want him to stop and to never, ever stop.

My mind is a bubbling contradiction. In the end, I go with it. I've already made it this far, and

I'll be damned if I call quits before making it over the finish line.

Even if I am forced to put my trust in him.

Suddenly, he pushes something cold and hard against my clit. The alternate sensation has my pussy weeping, begging, and then he flicks the toy on. Tingles spread through my body, all centered around the vibrating piece of magic at my core. I toss my head back, relishing in the storm building, savoring each climb of that wave. But before I can let loose and ride that glorious wave back to shore, he stops, pulling away.

The vibrator still hums in the room, but he's not touching me with it. He isn't touching me at all. The waves recede, slowly lapping instead of building. I squirm on the bed, trying to squeeze my thighs, rub on his face, anything to push me over the edge.

"Easy, Kitten. You don't come until I say so." He chuckles against the inside of my thigh and presses it back to my core. This time, the orgasm builds faster, rushing toward that crest. My hips gyrate, seeking more, but again he stops.

"Motherfucker. Stop this shit."

I don't know how many times he brings me to the edge and back. Sweat clings to my skin, and my flesh feels raw and overly sensitive. My body has betrayed me on the most basic level, refusing to crest that last hill and spiral into oblivion. He has complete and total control. At this point, I don't even care. I just want to fucking come.

Tears sting my eyes, and my throat is tight with the helpless sensation, but I refuse to break.

Pacey

chapter five

FUCK, she is the most beautiful woman I have ever seen. Every time I bring her to that edge, her body ignites, skin glistening, back arched, chest panting.

I've never wanted to consume someone so fucking badly.

She's so fucking close to breaking. I can sense the shift in her. Little does she know that is exactly why we did this. I want her completely, not half of her thinking about a silly picture on Instagram or lost in her thoughts. I want her crazed with desire. The only thoughts in that beautiful mind need to be of my cock and the pleasure I'm bringing her.

I should have known it would take a lot to bring her to this point. She likes to be in control. That was obvious after our first date. But she made a mistake today.

The moment she messaged me, I knew she wasn't as flippant about the encounter as she had led me to believe. She gave herself away asking about it earlier.

I'd bet my left nut that she has thought about that night every day since. As much as I have, if not more. Something spooked her, and I plan to find out what.

But first . . .

Settling between her thighs, I rub my cock up her slit. Precum mixes with the juices from her. Her breath pants out, her fingers digging into her palms where they are tied to the headboard. Fuck, I want to bury myself deep inside her, imprint the feel of my cock on her soul. Grabbing the base of my cock, I slap the head against her clit.

"Son of a—"

I slap it again before she can finish. This time, she's prepared. "Holy saints," she growls out. This time, when I run my dick through her wet slit, I slide inside.

"Fuck, your pussy feels good." Flexing my hips, I grind into her. "Do you like that? You like the way I own your pussy, Kitten?"

"Yes."

Lifting her ass, I pound every inch into her.

"Tell me how much you like it, baby. Let me hear you scream."

"Fuck. Fuck. Fuck!"

The walls of her pussy tighten around me, clenching my cock and making it damn near impossible to move, but I pull out before she tumbles over that precipice and slap my cock against her clit again.

Once.

Twice.

Three times.

Then I slide back inside her and drive my cock into her core.

"Pacey . . . Pacey."

Over and over, I slide in and then slap her pussy before sliding back in. On the third time I pull out, when I slap across her, she shatters. Her pussy pulses with the force of the orgasm, her juices spraying across my hand and my cock, soaking my sheets. My hand tightens at the base of my cock, squeezing, fighting the orgasm trying to rip through me.

She moans my name again, and the sound tears through me like a siren's call. My cock erupts, my seed spilling across her stomach . . . her chest.

Fuck, what is this woman doing to me?

Slipping back inside her, I fuck her sweet flesh

until my cock is spent, milked dry. Then I slide out and lean between her legs and proceed to lick her clean.

Somehow, the vixen manages to free a hand and proceeds to pull the blindfold from her eyes before freeing the other. Then her hands are in my hair, wrapping around my shoulders, pulling me up . . . up . . . up. Her mouth presses to mine, a moan escaping at her taste on my lips.

I lose myself in her. In that kiss. Nothing else matters but this moment and this woman. Pulling away, I stand and take the comforter with me. It's soaked, and there is no way it will keep either of us warm tonight. I toss it in a corner and pull open the closet door. Harriet watches me with a dazed expression on her face as I slip into the closet and return with another blanket.

Flipping it open, I cover her body and then crawl into the bed next to her.

"Shouldn't we shower? I–I mean," she stutters.

"No," I said with a grin stretching over my face.

Her eyes widen. "But—"

"Do you have a problem sleeping with my cum coating your flesh, Kitten?"

"No?" The answer sounds more like a question, and with each moment that passes, I can see the realization of what just occurred here sinking in. Pulling her lips to mine, I kiss it away.

"You are absolutely perfect. Now come here." Opening my arms, I pull her to my side. She nestles her head in the crook of my arm and closes her eyes.

I stare up at the ceiling as her breath evens out and her body goes limp against mine.

Fuck.

Never in my life has a woman dug under my skin and burrowed so deep. I've never been the type to date. I damn sure never wanted a girlfriend or marriage. As a child, I was forced to watch my mother bring home a different guy every other month. She was the type of woman who needed a man to make her feel loved. Something was broken inside her a long time ago, and unfortunately, she allowed each and every one of the men to break her more.

She believed wholeheartedly in soulmates. The problem was that she believed every man who showed her a lick of attention was her soulmate and poured everything she was into them. Then when they got tired of the clinginess or found something better, she was left brokenhearted.

Over and over again.

I was the only constant, but the love of a small

child wasn't what she needed. It didn't fill that void in her, so once the tears dried up, she put herself back out there and started the whole process over again.

I promised myself then that I wouldn't be the reason a woman broke. Fucking was one thing. One and done. But never would I lead a woman to believe I wanted more.

It's worked perfectly fine for me up until now.

Until this moment, while I lay in the bed holding Harriet and a future passed before my eyes. A future I never thought I would want.

But I can see it clearly now. She makes me want things I had given up on thirty years ago. She makes me want more.

harriet

chapter six

I ADJUST the focus on my camera one more time before holding it up and peering through the lens. Perfection.

The shutter clicks in rapid concession.

God, sometimes, it feels good to take a picture of something beautiful without the added pressure of being paid for the job. I forget that sometimes, that I love photography, and also all the reasons I first started.

Nowadays, I tend to mentally calculate how many images I need for each job in order to pay bills. The answer is too many.

Slowly, I was losing focus of my dream and almost dreading the work. But not today. Today, I am simply soaking in the beauty, and if I get a good picture, great. If not, oh, well. I needed this. Ever since I left Pacey's after a night of unexplainable sex, my mind has a been a mess.

That man did things to me that I have only read about in books, not fully understanding. By the end, I'm fairly certain I was in fact purring like the kitten he called me. But fuck.

As great as the sex was, and it was fucking fantastic, I still wasn't sure how I was supposed to face him again. I squirted all over his bed. All over him. Never in my life did I think my body would be capable of doing something like that. But under his careful guidance, it fucking gushed like a damn waterfall.

I had absolutely no control over it.

And that brings my thoughts back to why I needed this . . . this one moment away from every expectation and obligation. A single moment to just be. And hopefully, to sort out my tumbling thoughts.

I lost control.

It's never happened before. I've never allowed it to happen. But Pacey didn't give me an option, and I'll be damned, but I think I liked it. It also scared the fuck out of me.

There are three things I know about Pacey.

· · ·

(1) He knows how to play my body like a violin.

(2) He unnervingly has a way of making me trust him.

(3) He does not do relationships.

So why the hell does he keep texting me? Why do I have the distinct feeling that he wants more than either of us had agreed to? It can't happen. I won't let it. Kennady's voice echoes in my thoughts. "*You think you can make him fall in love?*"

Do I even want him to?

No. We're having fun. That's it. The first sign of something more, and I'm out.

O.U.T.

My phone vibrates in my back pocket. Letting my camera dangle around my neck, I pull it out and then spend an unhealthy amount of time reminding my heart that we don't do this racy, panicky thing when I see his name pop up.

Pacey: Dinner tonight, 7pm.

Me: That sounds like a good time for dinner.

I try to play it cool. Obviously, he's inviting me to dinner, but the man could at least ask. This is exactly what I mean about his taking control. Ask the question and give me the option to accept. Apparently, that goes against his belief system.

I can almost picture him smirking down at his phone, reading my message.

Pacey: Let me clarify. I would love to take you to dinner tonight.

Me: Hmmm. I suppose I should eat.

Pacey: How is 7pm?

Me: Where? I'll meet you there.

The three dots blink across the bottom for so long that I'm not sure he will reply. But the man is either really smart or desperate because the next message is just the name of a restaurant.

I pack up my camera and hike back to my car. The whole time, my fingers itch to text him again.

Thirty minutes later, I'm back home and unloaded. I plop down on the couch and open up Instagram. Somehow, I end up on Pacey's profile again, curiosity getting the best of me. But when I see the picture of him and the beautiful brunette again, my stomach sinks.

What the hell am I doing? Yes, he said I didn't need to worry about her. I run through the conversation in my mind. At no point did he say he wasn't seeing her or that she wasn't someone important to him.

And she's still there, pushed against his chest, his head nuzzling her hair. Her eyes are soft and so full of love and trust. I have photographed hundreds of people, and I know the eyes are where you look if you want the truth.

The truth is that regardless of what Pacey says, this woman is in love. Regardless of whether she hacked his phone or not, he knows about the photo and has left it up for the world to see. That means either he really cares about her, or he knows she would take issue if he took it down. Considering he just spent hours fucking me to the point of exhaustion, I'd say it's probably option two.

The truth settles on my shoulders, leaving a nasty, ashy taste in my mouth.

I need to put a stop to this before an innocent person gets hurt.

Swapping to my message app, I text him letting him know that something came up and I won't be able to make it. Then I delete the whole thread of messages and toss my phone on the couch beside me. It dings once, but I ignore it. The damn thing needs a little time out. And I need some space to come to terms with the fact that I have seriously fucked up.

one week
later

Pacey

chapter seven

IT'S A BEAUTIFUL EVENING. The restaurant Weston chose has a huge back deck filled with seating. Every inch of the wood is decorated with tiny bulbs of soft light. Past the deck, there is a walkway that leads to a pier, and past that, the moon glistens off the lake. Leaning against the railing, I breathe deeply, soaking in the sweet scent of night air.

I try to smile when Asher slaps my shoulder in greeting. Try being the keyword here. Don't get me wrong, I am over the fucking moon happy for Wes and Lucy. Their love story is one for the books, but even seeing Weston dropped to one knee and proposed to Lucy couldn't shake my shitty mood. Luckily, Ash doesn't hang around to chat.

Four dates.

Four stand-ups.

Four no-shows.

If I didn't know any better, I'd think Harriet was trying to blow me off. It damn sure seems that way. The problem is, I know she wants me. But for some godforsaken reason, she has avoided me for the last week.

The day after she came by my apartment, she was texting me constantly. She was fully invested in this thing between us, but something happened, and every day since, she has taken longer and longer to reply . . . if she replied at all.

Then earlier today, I saw a gorgeous photo of the clear blue sky through the top of a cluster of trees. I snapped a picture and sent it to her. I don't even know why, but something about the colors and abstract feel of the photo reminded me of her and I wanted to share it.

Thirty-one minutes later, she messaged back asking me to do her a favor. I jumped at the opportunity. Anything, if it meant seeing her again. Hell, I even replied back with the words, *Anything for you, kitten.*

And what did I get back?

Please lose my number.

What?

I was too shocked to reply, and then when I finally got my brain to wrap around the sentence, I couldn't. She asked to be left alone, and I'll be damned if I go against her wishes. Even if every fiber of my being wants to message her and ask *what the fuck?*

I had to force myself to not drive by her house and knock on the door.

Needless to say, my head isn't in the right space right now. Even the fact that my best friend just asked his girl to marry him can't push this cloud away.

"Are you alright?" Lucy says, placing a hand against my forehead. "No fever."

I swat her hand away. "What are you doing?"

"Checking to see if you're sick, dummy." Her brow is pinched with worry as she watches me.

"No, I'm not sick. Why would you say that?"

Lucy sighs and waves a hand around the space. "You're surrounded by tons of beautiful women, and not once have I seen you check one out." Placing a hand on her hip, she cocks her head to the side. "So, either you're sick or dead. Which is it?"

My shoulders slump. And here I thought I had fooled everyone. "I feel pretty dead," I admit.

Her eyes light with concern. "What happened?"

Somehow, I end up unloading the whole damn thing on her, and like a good friend, she listens to it all, even if she should be celebrating with her new fiancé. Damn, that's going to take some getting used to.

"Dang. That's rough, Pace. What are you going to do?" she asks, and damn if that isn't what I have been here contemplating myself.

"What can I do?" I growl. "She asked me to leave her alone, so I will. I won't text her or call her unless she reaches out first." Even if it fucking kills me.

"I'm sorry you're dealing with all this. I can tell you really like her."

I huff a dry laugh. "Yeah, I did."

Lucy pats my hand, and I can't help but notice the big ass diamond there now. If things had been different, would I have bought Harriet a diamond? Would it have looked like this?

"If there's anything I can do to help, just let me know."

I ponder that for a moment, then grab her hand in mine. "Lucy, you're a genius."

"I am?" Confusion is painted across her brow. She opens her mouth to say something else, but I interrupt her.

"I think I know how to get her to message me. We just need to do what you did last time." Grabbing a couple of flutes of champagne off our table,

I turn to her and hold one out. She wraps her hand around the stem.

"Pacey, I don't think that will work again," she hedges.

"Sure, it will. Come on, we have to at least try."

She shakes her head but steps closer. Holding up my phone, I snap a pic of us taking a sip of champagne together. Turning my phone around, I look at the picture and nod, then post it. My pulse is racing as I stare down at my phone, waiting for her text to come through. But nothing happens.

Lucy pats me on the arm and offers a small smile. "Maybe she hasn't seen it yet. Give it time."

Nodding, I pull up her profile and try to see if she is online, but I don't know how to do all that, so I just click on the last picture she posted and try to will her to text me.

"Is that her?" Lucy asks, taking my phone.

"Yeah, that's her main profile. She has another for her business."

"Oh, what does she do?"

"She's a photographer. Here, let me show you."

Pulling my phone back, I type in her other profile name and pass it back. I wonder what Harriet would think if she knew I showed this profile off to anyone who gave me the chance. Kid having a birthday party? I know an amazing photographer.

"Oh, these are amazing. She's really good."

My chest swells in pride even though I didn't take the pictures. It's pride in Harriet and everything she has accomplished that fills me now. Lucy passes my phone back and grins. "I think I have an idea."

"Really? What?" I try to keep the pleading out of my voice, but at this point, I will take any help I can get. That woman has dug herself in deep, and I don't know how to let her go.

Lucy winks before catching Weston's eye. He raises a hand, waving her over, but she turns to me before leaving. "I'll tell you if it works out. I don't want you to get your hopes up."

I don't bother arguing. Over the last three years, I've learned that when Lucy makes her mind up about something, you can't change it. But a part of me is already clinging to that small shred of hope.

harriet

chapter eight

I SEE the photo as soon as I wake. It's become some kind of obsession to scroll social media first thing in the morning. I've never hated the app more than I do right this moment.

Even though I told myself to let him go, what I know I should do and what I want to do seem to be warring within me. I don't know how long I stare at the photo, zooming in to try to pick apart the woman in the picture. But she is beautiful, and honestly, it isn't her fault that I got tangled up with Pacey. If anything, I am the devil in their story.

Then I see the diamond glaring at me on her ring finger. Scrolling down, I check the other photo. No ring.

Did he propose to her? Is that . . . am I . . .? I feel like I'm losing my mind here, overanalyzing every single conversation I've had with him and comparing it with what I see in front of my face. If Kennady and I were on speaking terms, I would call her and ask if she knows this girl. But we haven't spoken more than a handful of words since that evening at her apartment.

My phone rings, startling me. I don't recognize the number, but it's local, so I answer.

"Hello?"

"Hi, can I speak to Harriet Banks, please?"

"This is she. How can I help you?"

"Oh, perfect. I was wondering if you had any availability for a custom photo shoot the weekend of the 13th?"

"I believe so. Can I place you on hold for just a moment and check my calendar?"

"Of course."

Muting the conversation, I pull up my calendar and double-check the date even though I know I don't have anything scheduled. A fact I had been worrying over relentlessly for the last few weeks. It's been a rough few months.

"Okay. It looks like I'm free that weekend. What do you have in mind?"

"Oh, yay! That's great. Pacey showed me your page, and I just knew you would be perfect for the job. Your work is phenomenal."

My heart lurches in my chest when she

mentions Pacey's name. The same way it does any time I think his name or see something that reminds me of him. But this morning, it hurts a little more.

"So, we've rented out the Winter Park Resort in Colorado for engagement photos. We will provide a room, and all amenities will be paid, including flight and car rental."

Engagement photos. Engagement photos. Engagement photos.

Those two words play on repeat in my mind. Over and over. The image of the gorgeous brunette with a flashy diamond ring flashes before my eyes. I don't hear the rest of what she says. I can't focus. This is the woman in the photo, and Pacey told her I was a photographer. She wants to hire me to take pictures of her engagement.

I mumble a few yeses and then rattle off my email when she requests it.

She knows. She has to know. Otherwise, why would she request me out of all the photographers in the area?

Unless she doesn't know, and she genuinely wants someone good. Pacey recommended me, and she trusts him, so she didn't ask any questions.

Either way, I can't take the job. There isn't any way I'll be able to snap photos of them together

SUTTON SNOW & TINLEY BLAKE

and not recall every touch of his on my body. My phone dings with an email. Opening it, I read through the recap of our conversation, already forming my own reply and reluctant refusal, when I reach the compensation portion of the email. My eyes widen.

Surely, that's a typo.

But no, it's repeated again, and . . . holy saints. This will more than cover expenses for half a fucking year.

That settles it. I'm taking the job. For that much money, I can be professional. I can be the most professional person in the whole damn universe. I will pop in, pretend Pacey doesn't exist, and take some amazing photos. Then I'll fly home and forget that man ever existed.

That settled, I open the contract, sign on the dotted line, and email it back over to . . . Lucy.

Lucy.

It feels good to put a name and voice to the woman in the photos. And from the brief conversation with her, she seems like a genuinely nice person. It makes it a lot harder to ignore her existence.

Pacey

chapter nine

FOR FUCK'S SAKE, I'll never understand why Lucy wanted to do this shit here. It's only October and already colder as shit. I can't imagine having a wedding up here in March. Rent a space back home and pay someone to fill the place with fake snow. We can make it work. But this is what she wants, and Weston always makes sure Lucy gets what she wants.

"Pace! You made it," Lucy says, pulling me in for a quick hug. She flew in last night before everyone else and got everything arranged for the day. Weston, unfortunately, wasn't able to join her right away, so I bumped up my flight and got here as quickly as I could so she wouldn't be alone.

"Of course I made it. Did you doubt me?" I smirk down at her beanie-clad head. Her nose is pink from the chill in the air, but it only makes her cuter. Like a little toddler. Adorable.

"Nah, not a bit. I knew you would make it happen," she says, glancing up at me with a mischievous grin.

"For you? Always."

We step back inside the lobby, and I spend a few minutes trying to rub some warmth back into my hands. Luckily, the inside is warm and toasty, so it doesn't take long before I can feel my fingers again. Never again will I leave my coat packed in my suitcase. I don't care how much room it takes up in the carry-on.

"Speaking of making things happen. I know I told you not to get your hopes up, but it looks like my plan might work."

"You mean . . ." I try to keep the hope out of my tone, but I know I don't fool her.

"Yep. She should be here any minute. Now it's up to you to not fuck this up again," she says, narrowing her eyes.

I pick her up and spin in a circle. Her laughter echoes off the walls of the thankfully empty lobby. "You are amazing. Remind me to buy you something pretty when we get back home."

"I'll hold you to that."

Setting her on the ground, I drape my arm

across her shoulder. My mood is considerably lighter than it has been in weeks. I don't know what magic Lucy used to pull this off, but I'm grateful.

"Excuse me? Lucy?" I spin around, pulling Lucy with me, and come face to face with the woman who has haunted my thoughts for the last three weeks. Lucy lifts a hand, offering it to Harriet.

"Hi, you must be Harriet. It's great to finally meet you. I've heard so many wonderful things."

Harriet's eyes cut to me and narrow briefly before glancing back to Lucy. "It's great to meet you too. This place is beautiful."

"It is. I've always dreamed of a snowy wedding, and this place was at the top of my venue picks. By the time the wedding gets here, the mountains will be covered."

"I'm sure it will be perfect," Harriet says with a small smile.

I watch the two women exchange words, waiting for Harriet to acknowledge my presence, but she seems content to ignore me altogether. When there is a break in the flow of conversation, I insert myself.

"It's good to see you, Harriet. You look great."

Her eyes flash with irritation before she buries

it down deep. "Pacey." She nods hello. Fucking nods her head and then continues pretending I don't exist. That just won't do.

"How was your flight?" I ask, refusing to let her cut this off.

"Cozy," she deadpans.

Fucking hell, she really doesn't want to make this easy. But I promised not to text the girl. I didn't say a damn thing about talking to her in public.

"Did you need help finding your room? If so, I'm happy to show you the way." Never mind the fact that I just walked in and don't even know where my own room is. I'll figure it out, and if by some chance we get lost while looking, well, that's just more time alone with her.

She narrows her gaze at me, but I ignore that. At least she's finally looking at me. "That's not necessary."

"Would you like a drink? Maybe we can catch up?" I offer.

"No." Her answer leaves no room for convincing. It's final. But I refuse to be pushed away.

Lucy slips under my arm and offers a small smile of encouragement before stepping over to the lobby desk. Glancing back at Harriet, I try to gauge her mood, but she's so closed off to me. It's like there's a stranger standing in front of me wearing the skin of the woman I know. Reaching for her hand, I lift it to my lips and press a kiss to her knuckles. "You really do look amazing. Almost good enough to eat."

She snatches her hand back, a blush rising to her cheeks. "You have a lot of fucking nerve."

"Wow, Kitten, put those claws away. I just wanted to catch up," I say with a smirk.

Her hands clench into a fist. "Do not touch me. Do not speak to me. I am here for a job, not to play catch-up with you. As far as I'm concerned, this" —she waves a hand between us— "never happened. We are not a thing, and never will be. Now go back to your fiancée before I lose the last grip I have on my control and tell her exactly what kind of man she is marrying."

I'm left stunned speechless as she spins on her heel and storms away.

Needless to say, I didn't see that happening. It takes way longer than I'm willing to admit to pick my jaw up off the floor and make my way back to Lucy. Leaning down, I whisper in her ear. Her eyes widen as what Harriet said sinks in.

"Oh, Pacey. She thinks . . . how? Why?" Lucy asks.

I grimace at the thought of how Harriet must

see me. "I don't know, but she stormed off before I could set her straight."

"Well, at least now you know why she pulled back."

"Yeah." The grin stretching across my face feels foreign. But I can't help it. I thought I did something wrong, something to push her away. I've racked my brain for weeks trying to figure out where I went wrong, when all along, it was a simple misunderstanding.

"Oh, no. I know what that grin means. You're about to do something stupid, aren't you?"

"Who, me? Never," I singsong as I take my keycard and head in the direction of the elevator.

Lucy follows behind me with a shake of her head. "Right. What was I thinking?"

harriet

chapter Ten

THAT SON OF A BITCH. He is either the stupidest or the bravest bastard I know. Who the hell makes those kinds of comments while his fiancée is right there? Does she not know? Or not care? Either way, I can't wait to get this job over and get my ass back home and as far away from Pacey Roberts as possible.

I stab my finger into the elevator button and tap my foot while waiting for the doors to open. I almost lost it. It took everything in me to not march over to Lucy right then and tell her exactly the type of person that Pacey is. God, I wanted to. But then this job would be over, and honestly, I need the money.

The doors open with a whoosh. Stepping inside, I give myself until I reach my floor to be angry. In those few minutes, I imagine all the things I wish I could say and do to him, starting with knocking that sexy ass smirk from his face. When the doors open again, I take a deep breath, and as I step from the elevator, I let it go.

I let him go.

Swiping my card at the door, I step inside and open my suitcase. Pulling up the itinerary on my phone, I see we're supposed to be at lunch in less than thirty minutes. I pull up the location of the restaurant and then dig through my clothes for a heavy sweater.

I still don't understand the reason I'm needed at these locations unless Lucy wants the entire trip documented. Normally, we would select a specific area and pose for photos, and I would be done. But she sent over a detailed itinerary with instructions on when and where to be. God knows, the woman is paying me enough. The least I can do is show up.

Hell, I'll cover every minute of this trip if she wants.

I slip the sweater over my head and slide on a pair of warm booties before checking my makeup and hair in the mirror. Five minutes later, I'm standing back in front of the elevator, my head lifted, back straight, camera dangling around my neck, and I'm determined to not allow Pacey to affect me anymore.

It takes fifteen minutes for me to find the restaurant and another five to locate their table. The group of people has tripled in size in the last half hour. Everyone is sitting around a table in the back, laughing and giggling. I pause, lifting my camera, and snap a few candid shots of them.

Just as I finish, a man brushes past me, almost knocking into me. Clenching my fist, I bite back a snarky comment and follow him. I'm less than six feet away when he reaches the table. I watch as he steps up behind Lucy and Pacey, wraps his hands in Lucy's hair, tugs her head back, and then lays his mouth over hers.

My feet stop moving. I'm almost positive if some snapped a photo of me right now, my jaw would be on the ground.

The kiss goes on way too long to be anything but romantic. When the man finally peels his face from Lucy's, he turns to Pacey and the two hug.

They hug.

Like . . . like . . . I don't fucking know what.

I stumble forward, pasting a smile to my face. *Professional.* I'm a fucking pro. Even if I am losing my ever-loving mind internally. Everything I thought I knew just flew out the window, and now I'm second-guessing everything.

Every. Single. Thing.

Pacey is the first to notice me. I meet his gaze for a brief second and cut my gaze back to Lucy. This is too much. I need answers and I need them now, because if there is a chance that I was wrong . . . even the smallest chance that Pacey isn't a sleazebag, cheating piece of shit, then I need to know.

Now.

So, I do what any professional woman who is on the hunt for answers does. I fake it until I make it.

"How about we get a few photos of the happy couple?" I ask the group, smiling my best smile.

It quickly drops from my face when Pacey, Lucy, and the new guy stand up together. I swallow my shock and point to a space a few feet away that will make a great backdrop. Thankfully, when I step back to line up the camera, Pacey follows, confirming that the new guy is in fact with Lucy.

Lifting my camera, I adjust the lens and snap a few pictures before switching the settings up. Pacey stands nearby, watching my every move. At one point, I glance up at him to see him studying the camera with an unrelenting focus.

"What are you doing?" I ask.

His full lips spread into a sinful grin. "I'm just

trying to make sure I know how to use that camera for later."

"For later?"

His grin melts away, replaced with his panty-melting smirk that has my core tightening. "Yeah. How else would I take pictures of you spread beneath me, my cum glistening between your thighs?"

I almost drop my camera right there. I'm pretty sure an audible squeak escapes through my pressed lips. The things this man says to me should be illegal. Lock him up and toss away the key. On second thought, give me the key. I need a way to let him out so he can follow through every delicious thought he has.

It's only fair. He had me tied to his bed, after all. I should get the chance to repay the favor. My pulse races, my heart galloping full speed ahead in my chest as he steps closer, running the pad of his finger down the side of my arm.

"You'd like that, wouldn't you, Kitten?" His voice is like velvet. I want to fall into it, bask in the warmth of his body, and let him have his way with me.

Shaking my head to clear my thoughts, I reply, "Huh?" I know. I know. Not the best comeback, but shit.

"I can see the excitement in your eyes, the flush of your skin. The idea of me documenting the things I want to do with your body turns you on."

"I–I . . . I need a new SD card. I'll be back."

I flee, racing away as fast as my legs will carry me. Which, mind you, is not very fast since they are a quivering mess.

Pacey

chapter eleven

I STAND THERE with a shit-eating grin on my face for all of five minutes before I follow Harriet. A part of me wants to give her a few minutes to collect herself. I know seeing Weston and finally understanding just how wrong she was about mine and Lucy's relationship had to be jarring for her. Anyone in their right mind would need a minute to process that, but if I have learned anything this last month, it's when it comes to Harriet, if I give her space and time to get in her own thoughts, she will run.

No more running.

We are going to face whatever the hell this is between us head on and let the pieces fall where they will.

Jumping on the elevator, I press her floor button and run through the things I want to say to her. The things I'm dying to do to her. Starting with spanking that perfect ass for running from me and not taking five minutes to talk this shit out weeks ago.

The elevator dings, and the doors glide open slowly. I lift my head and meet Harriet's gaze. Her eyes widen when she sees me standing there, and I can almost see her thoughts play across her face.

After a moment of hesitation, she steps onto the elevator, her camera dangling from a cord around her neck. I don't bother moving out of her way. Her lush ass brushes against the front of my pants as she turns to face the front. The sweet scent of lilacs fills the small enclosure, lighting my blood on fire. Leaning forward, I brush the hair away from her neck and run my nose along her neck. Her skin pebbles from the contact.

"What are you doing?" Her words come out as a breathless moan.

"What do you want me to do?" I tease.

"Nothing."

"I think that's a lie," I say, pressing my hard cock against her ass. Her hand reaches back, palming me through my pants as she tilts her head to the side, offering me easier access to her neck.

"You feel what you do to me, Kitten? Just

being in the same room with you has me hard as a rock."

"That seems like a personal problem."

Spinning her around, I hit the emergency stop on the elevator and press my mouth to hers. She opens for me immediately, her tongue darting out to meet mine. Gripping her hips, I pull her body flush to mine, savoring the feel of her in my arms once again.

"That's where you're wrong. You ran away. You made me wait weeks to taste your sweet flesh again. And for what?"

"I thought—" she whimpers.

"I know what you thought. That doesn't matter now. Now, you're going to make it up to me."

"I am?"

Unzipping my pants, I pull my cock free. It bobs in the air between us. Her hand reaches forward, her fingers running along the length before wrapping tightly around it.

Lifting the camera from around her neck, I slip it over my head and pop the screen cover off. "Yes, you are. And if you're a good girl, I might even slide it into that tight pussy before we reach the lobby. Now get on your knees and show me how sorry you are."

Her eyes flash with anger, and fuck if I don't like the idea of torturing her slowly until she gives me what I want, but then she drops to her knees. Her breath is hot against the head of my cock, and then her tongue slips out and traces a circle around the tip before opening her mouth and taking me in.

Lifting the camera, I power it on and snap a photo of her lips encircling my cock. She glances up at me, her eyes lust-filled. I press the shutter button again and again.

My balls tighten as she runs her hand up and down my cock in sync with her mouth. It takes everything I have in me to not spill my load right this second. Wrapping my hand through her hair, I tug her head forward, fucking the back of her throat until she gags around my cock. Tears run down her cheeks, but she doesn't pull away.

"Fuck, that's a good girl. Take my cock, Kitten."

Her moans fill the small space, the sound vibrating against the tip. Her free hand slips between her legs, rubbing against the fabric of her jeans across her pussy. Fuck.

"You want me to fuck that tight pussy, baby?"

Her only answer is to swallow my cock deeper in her mouth.

Pulling my cock from her mouth, I rub the head across her swollen pink lips and snap another picture. Her tongue dips out, licking at the tip, lapping at the precum dripping from my cock like a fucking Kitten lapping milk from a dish.

"Stand up and pull your jeans down."

Her eyes dart to the number board and back to mine. I raise an eyebrow, waiting to see what she decides. We've been stopped on this elevator for at least five minutes now, and someone is sure to notice soon. Glancing up, I check the space for a camera and grin when I see a small red dot in the top right corner.

Harriet stands, pulling her jeans down to the middle of her thighs. The shirt she has on still covers her, hiding her from viewing eyes.

For now.

Spinning her around, I push her shoulder forward and line my cock up with her entrance. But before I push inside her, I take a take another photo of my cock pressed against the swell of her ass. She's soaking wet, her juices coating her sweet pussy. If I had more time, I'd drop to my knees and swallow every drop.

Leaning forward, I whisper in her ear, "Let's put on a good show for the camera, Kitten." She tenses, but I don't give her a chance to reply before shoving inside her.

"Fuck, you feel good. I should spank that perky ass for the shit you pulled." The walls of her pussy clench around me as I slowly pull out, pressing the shutter button repeatedly. Once the final rung of my ladder is free, I shove back into her . . . hard.

"This pussy is mine."

"You're mine."

Each word is punctuated by a punishing thrust that brings me closer and closer to the edge of oblivion.

"Understand?" I growl, grinding my hips into her ass.

"Fuck," Harriet pants. Her head is thrown back, her hands clenching the bar running the length of the elevator wall. Gripping her hips, I lift her, angling her body so I can fuck her harder.

"I said" —thrust— "do you understand?" —thrust—

"*Yes.*" She groans as I fuck her tight pussy.

"Say it," I grind out, fighting to hold off my own release.

"Fuck you."

I slow my pace, dragging out the impending orgasm until she gives me what I want. "I can play your body like the finest instrument, Kitten, and I will. Unless you say the words. Give me what I want, and I'll make this pussy purr."

"Never."

I pump into her harder and harder. Her body is strung tightly, just begging to be pushed over the edge, and I know just how to make it happen, but she wants to play hard. Which is fine. In the end, I'll win. She just doesn't know it yet.

"Fine, have it your way, darlin'."

With a final thrust, my orgasm rushes through me, pumping into her. My body shakes with the force of it, my legs trembling. Harriet whines low in her throat, wiggling her ass against me, but I still my hips and pull free from her delicious warmth. Tugging my pants back up, I hit the elevator stop button and grab the bar as it shifts back into motion.

Harriet spins around, her eyes flashing with rage, before slipping her jeans back up and narrowing her gaze. I snap a picture of her flushed face and the storm brewing in her eyes before I turn to face the front of the elevator just as the doors open.

harriet

chapter Twelve

THE ENTIRE WALK back to the restaurant is
filled with tense silence. Every fiber of my being
wants to lash out at him, to wipe that cocky as fuck
smirk right off his chiseled face. But doing so
would let him know just how much his little stunt
affected me, and I'm not about to let that happen.
So I bear it.

Every step I take causes an uncomfortable
wetness to fill my panties. The fucker didn't just
withhold my orgasm. A fucking orgasm I was just
about to crest. No. He made sure to fucking finish
himself. His cum fills my panties, coating every
inch of my pussy.

Lucy's gaze meets mine, then ticks to Pacey's
before returning to scan my face. I force a smile to
my face as I pull out a chair and sit. Luckily, we
weren't gone too long. Just long enough for Pacey

to use my body for his own gain and leave me hanging. Drinks have been served, and a couple of appetizers line the table, but the menus are still there, so at least I didn't miss the chance to eat too.

Wouldn't that be my luck?

Pacey pulls out a chair next to me and sits. I toss a narrowed look his way before picking up my menu. Fucker.

All because I wouldn't say what he wanted to hear. I knew the man was a control freak in the bedroom, but this is taking it to a whole new level. Isn't there some kind of guy code against leaving a woman unsatisfied? If not, there should be.

Not that he would care. The fucker probably got off on the idea of it.

Literally.

The proof is currently coating the insides of my thighs.

Crossing my legs, I set the menu down and pick up my glass of water, taking a small sip, and pull myself out of my own head and pay attention to the conversation around me. After seeing Weston with Lucy, I wonder how I ever thought she and Pacey were engaged. The two are clearly in love. Their bodies are constantly touching, and every few minutes, they share a glance with each other, accompanied by a blush stealing across

Lucy's cheeks. I squirm in my seat, trying to get comfortable while stealing a glance at Pacey.

"You look a little uncomfortable there. Anything I can help you with?" Pacey says into my ear.

"You've done enough, thanks."

"Tell me what I want to hear, and I'll take you back to the room right this second and lick your pussy clean." His words send a shiver down my spine, but I refuse to give in.

"And then what?" I ask. The thought of his head between my legs leaves me breathless.

"Whatever you want. But I'd start by finishing what I started in that elevator. Only this time, I think I'd take my time worshiping every inch of your body."

Turning to face him, I don't bother whispering anymore. If he wants to have this conversation in a crowded room, then so be it.

"And then what, Pacey? I like a good tumble in the sheets as much as the next girl, but I've had that. It was a great tumble, but—"

"You misunderstand, Kitten. I don't just want your body. I want you. All of you. I want to hear you say you are mine. Only mine."

His declaration shocks me. Kennedy led me to believe that this man never settled down. That he was a hit it and quit it kind of guy. Even when everything he has done and said proved otherwise, that thought kept curling in the back of my mind. "But—"

"No buts. Yes, or no?" he demands.

I think about it for approximately ten seconds. But let's be honest, we both know I want him. And according to him, he wants me too. My mind made up, I grin and say, "It depends."

"On what?" he asks suspiciously.

I take his hand in mine and stand. "On whether you're a good boy and follow through on your promise."

His answering grin makes my core tighten with need. He stands, mumbling an excuse to the table for our early departure, and then pulls me back through the restaurant.

"I called it," I hear Lucy exclaim behind me. "I'll have dinner sent up. I have a feeling you're going to need it."

Pacey chuckles under his breath as he leads me up to his room, which naturally is one door down from my own. I'm starting to suspect that Lucy knew exactly what she was doing when offering me this contract. And not all of it was for the photos I was paid to take. I mention as much to Pacey as the door closes behind us.

"Lucy is a sneaky devil. I've spoken to her about you, and before you ask, no, she wouldn't have hired you just to get us in the same place. She really loved your work when I showed her," he says.

"So you did show her my work?" I ask as I kick off my heels by the door.

"Damn right. I show it to anyone who will listen."

"Why?" I don't know why I need to hear this right now, but I do. The thought of him showing off my work to random people makes my chest ache, and not in a bad way, but in a way I haven't experienced before. I rub the heel of my hand against the spot, trying to push it away.

Pacey pulls my hand away and wraps his arm around my waist, tugging me closer. "Because it's fucking good, that's why."

I glance up at him. "And you didn't know I was going to be here?"

He shakes his head, the soft light of the room catching on the lens of the camera with the movement. "Not until about five minutes before you walked in."

"And you were upset?" I press forward, intending to get this all out of the way now. No more misunderstandings. No more unasked questions.

"Why the fuck would I be upset? You told me to lose your number—which, by the way, was fucked up. I couldn't text you, couldn't call, but if you were here, I knew I could get you to talk to me. Even if I had to piss you off first." He chuckles.

"I really thought you were a piece of shit, fucking me while dating her." Pulling away, I slap his arm. "You could have told me when I asked about the picture."

"Hindsight, Kitten. If I had known what you were thinking, I would have, but at the time . . ."

"I get it. For what it's worth, it sucked for me too."

It feels good to get all this out in the open and discuss it like grown ass adults. I should have done this weeks ago instead of ghosting him, but everything Kennady had told me was running on repeat in my mind. The more I get to know him, the less I believe a word she said. I want to ask him, to come clean about her and the pact we made even if I have moved past that. I might have gone on that first date with him for her, but everything that has happened since then has been because I genuinely enjoy spending time with him.

I open my mouth to tell him everything, but he steps forward and presses a finger to my lips.

Lifting the camera from around his neck, he places it on the bed next to us. "I must not be doing this right if you're still able to think and speak."

I shut my mouth and lose myself in the feel of his skin against mine. It may be my imagination, but when he kisses me now, it feels more tender, gentler, as if he really is taking his time and worshiping my body. His fingers expertly unbutton my jeans and slip them down my thighs, along with my soaking wet panties. I step out of them and into his arms.

My shirt joins the rest of my clothes in a pile on the floor, and then he lays me back on the bed. His lips trail a path up one side of my body and down the other. Grabbing the camera, I focus on his hands and snap a picture, wanting to savor this moment forever. His fingers gently caress the path behind them. My breath hitches in my chest as his mouth descends between my thighs.

His gaze meets the camera as his tongue licks across my clit. I click the shutter, snapping multiple photos of the movement.

Within seconds, I'm writhing on the bed, sheets tangled in my grip. When he suckles my clit into his mouth and flicks my sensitive little nub, I shatter. Stars dance behind my lids. Noise ceases to exist, sucked into oblivion along with all other sense of time and space. I feel nothing, hear nothing, see nothing but his tongue as he licks through my quivering center.

Slowly, the world comes back into focus. The drum of my heartbeat in my ears fades, leaving me shaken to my core.

"Mmm, that's my girl."

"Yes," I reply.

Pacey

chapter Thirteen

I KISS my way back up her body, paying special attention to the glorious peaks across her chest. Fuck, she's perfect. Every inch of her begs for my touch. I can't decide where to start. I want to spend every second of every day consuming her.

Never in my life have I wanted someone the way I want her. It's not just physical, although that is phenomenal. But her mind, her morals. The way she carries herself and the spark of ire that lights her eyes when I say something that pisses her off. I want to spend the rest of my days finding ways to anger her just so I can see that spark and then fuck that heat out of her.

I don't know what tomorrow will bring, but I know I want to find out with her by my side. And for the first time since I met her, I believe it might be possible. We put it all on the table tonight and cleared the air. Now, right this second, is a fresh start. A new beginning.

I plan on making sure she enjoys every second of it.

"Do you feel thoroughly worshiped yet, Kitten?"

"Hmm. You're on the right track."

"Ah, so not quite fulfilled yet. Let's see what we can do about that," I say, sliding into her. Her legs are pressed to each side of my head, resting on my shoulders. I lean forward and fully settle inside her.

"How's that, Princess?"

"More."

She doesn't have to ask me twice. I thrust my hips, pounding into her with each pass. With each stroke, her moans grow louder. The words coming out of her mouth become less and less tangible until only one word is on repeat.

"Fuck. Fuck. Fuck."

I slam into her over and over, her chants a song of encouragement. When I feel her walls tightening around me, I slide a hand between her thighs and circle her clit with my thumb. Her legs squeeze together around my head, her fingers digging into my thighs.

I ride that first wave with her, her pussy

squeezing my cock so tight I don't know how I don't come. When her legs loosen around my shoulders, I slow my pace before easing out of her and flipping her onto her stomach. Straddling her thighs, I slide my cock back into her warm center. At this angle, I can feel every breath she takes, every silky pulse of her pussy.

"Is this sweet pussy mine now, Kitten?" I groan as I glide in and out of her.

"Yes." She moans, her head buried in a pillow.

I wrap my hand in her hair, tugging her hair and pulling her head back. "Let me hear you say it." With my cock fully seated inside her, I grind my pelvis into her ass and roll my hips. "You're mine."

Her breath pants out as I lose myself in the feel of her body. "I'm yours."

The words ring through me, settling in my bones, filling me with such indescribable pride that I want to shout from the rooftops. Instead, I pull Harriet to her knees and press a hand between her shoulder blades. She arches her back, pressing her ass into the air. Gripping her hips, I slide my cock out and push back inside her. Her moans echo around the room, filling the space.

"Good girl. Now come on my cock, Kitten."

Removing one hand, I trace the crack of her

ass. When the tip of my finger reaches her forbidden hole, I add a little pressure without entering her. She groans and bucks her hips. Spitting on the puckered hole, I rub my thumb through the moisture and slip inside her, inch by glorious inch.

She shatters around me. The pulsing grip of her pussy pulls my own orgasm from me. I pump into her, coating her silken walls with my seed until we both fall to the bed with a sigh. After a few moments to collect my breath, I sit up and grab the camera where she discarded it. Standing on shaking legs, I spread her legs wide and snap a picture of her glistening pussy. When she rolls over, I step back and get a picture of her whole body before zooming in to snap one of my cum coating her thighs.

With a grin, I set the camera on the nightstand and climb back in the bed beside her. "I knew I would need those lessons," I say, pressing a kiss to her lips.

harriet

chapter fourteen

I SPENT the entire weekend with Pacey in Colorado. After that first night, he did his best to keep me in the bed, but I managed to convince him to leave.

I had a job to do, after all, and I wasn't about to give that up for some dick.

Even if it was the best fucking dick I've ever had.

We ended up being on the same flight home. It was wonderful. Magical, even. Walking in the door to my house, I feel lighter and happier than I have in . . . well, I don't know how long. I don't remember a time I ever felt like this. For as long as I can recall, I have maintained strict control in every aspect of my life. And then I met Pacey.

He builds me up and makes me feel like the

most amazing woman in the world, like I can literally slay fucking dragons in heels and red lipstick.

But he doesn't give an inch in the bedroom. I didn't think I'd like it. And I was right. I fucking love it. There is something about having a man completely control my every move and not having to think or move or say a word unless he says so that is freeing and intoxicating.

Kicking off my shoes, I throw my purse on the kitchen counter and pull my computer from my carry-on. I had planned to edit the photos while in Colorado, but every free second I had was spent in a tangle of bodies with Pacey. Not that I'm complaining.

In fact, I peer at my watch. He's supposed to be back here in less than three hours. Sliding the SD card into my computer, I start the process of uploading all the pictures. While that works, I strip out of my clothes and climb into the shower.

I spend the better part of twenty minutes standing under the spray of hot water. It feels so good to be home. When the water starts to cool, I wash my hair and body and climb out. Wrapping a towel around my waist, I head to the kitchen to check on the progress and run straight into Kennady.

She's standing at the bar, watching the

slideshow of photos as they scroll across the screen. I open my mouth to ask what she's doing here when a photo of my mouth wrapped around Pacey's cock slides across the screen, followed by another of him sliding his cock into the crease of my ass.

Fuck. I forgot those were on there. Fuck. Fuck. Fuck.

Neither of us says a word until a photo of Pacey with his head between my thighs appears. I took this one after wrangling the camera from his hands. You can clearly see his face as he peers up at me.

"You fucking bitch."

"Kennady—"

"Don't try to lie your way out of this. The proof is in the picture, right? And you have more than a few of those."

"I wasn't going to lie. I have no reason to lie to you."

"No reason? You're fucking my boyfriend behind my back!"

"Pacey isn't your boyfriend, Kennady. You know that."

"And I suppose you think he's yours? You don't know a thing about him. He will fuck you and move on. That's all he knows."

I shrug my shoulders. "If he does, he does. It's my business. Not yours."

"Fuck you. I should have known you would try to steal him for yourself. You always think you're so much better than me. Well, don't come crying to me when he breaks your heart the way he did mine."

She doesn't give me a chance to reply before storming out the door. Grabbing my robe, I wrap it around my shoulders and step outside to grab the spare key. I should have moved it weeks ago, but I honestly didn't think she would come back around. We left things pretty shitty the last time we spoke, and after the things she said to me, I had zero interest in speaking to her again.

That task accomplished, I head back inside to get dressed and start edits. Grabbing my phone, I pull up Pacey's messages to tell him everything about Kennady, but something stops me. This is a conversation to have in person, not over text. I learned that lesson the hard way last time. Besides, he'll be here shortly. I'll come clean then.

After a few minutes, I lose myself in the process of choosing photos and moving them to a different folder. I store all the ones of Pacey and me separately and spend more time than I want to admit looking through them. All the while,

Kennady's words play over and over in the back of my mind. Even though we cleared the air in Colorado, we didn't really discuss much else. I've never been one of those girls who needed a label on a relationship. And I meant what I said. If he leaves and never looks back, I'll survive that.

Even if the thought of it feels like a punch to the gut.

Pacey

chapter fifteen

I'VE JUST SAT DOWN and ordered a beer when I feel an arm wrap around my shoulders. Spinning in my seat, I find a tiny blonde standing there.

"Kennady?"

"Hey, sexy. Miss me?"

"I haven't seen you lately."

"Well, I'm here now, baby," she says, running a hand down the top of my arm. I turn my body, angling away from her, but that doesn't deter her for long.

"You look tired. Why don't we get out of here?" Her hand rubs across my thigh and presses against my crotch. I reach down and take it into my own.

"Stop. I've told you I'm not interested."

"Oh, come on, baby. I'll show you a good time."

"It's not happening. I'm not available."

"Of course. How could I forget about your precious Harriet? Who do you think told her about you? She only dated you because I convinced her to. It was our little secret revenge plot."

Her words hit me like a freight train, forcing the air from my lungs. It can't be true. Harriet would have said something. What reason did she have for wanting revenge against me? I think back over every interaction I've had with Harriet. She's never given the slightest clue that she wasn't interested, that this was a game for her.

It's a lie.

"Aw, you didn't think she actually wanted you, did you?" She laughs. "Go on, run over there and ask her. But don't be surprised if she doesn't let you in."

Some bullshit Kennady made up to push me away from Harriet. I don't know why the girl won't leave me the hell alone. I've never given her any reason to think I wanted her. Quite the opposite. From the first time I met her, there was something about her that seemed shady. I couldn't pinpoint exactly what it was, but I trusted my gut.

The first time she tried to hook up, I let her down easily. It wasn't her fault that I had a weird feeling about her. But then she tried again and again. She started showing up at every restaurant I frequented. At the local bars when she thought I would be there. Eventually, I got fed up with it and told her there wasn't a chance in hell. When that didn't work, I started ignoring her.

I thought I was finally free. I haven't seen her in over a month, but if what she says is true, that's because she and Harriet hatched a plan to fuck with me. A fucking game where no one wins.

Glancing at my phone, I check the time. It's still a little early, but I need answers. Tossing a twenty on the bar, I slide my phone into my pocket and grab my keys. Ten minutes later, I pull into Harriet's drive.

Taking a deep breath, I knock on the door. The seconds tick by with alarming slowness as I wait for her to open the door, wondering if Kennady was telling the truth and she really won't see me. Then the door swings open and all thought leaves my mind.

Harriet smiles and beckons me inside. She's wearing a pair of short, tight shorts that hug her frame and an oversized tee. Her hair is on her head in a bun, small pieces falling free and framing her face. I've never seen her look more delectable. I step inside, letting the door close behind me.

When she turns back to face me, I grab her bun and tilt her head to the side as I pin her against the door. My mouth descends on hers, hard and unrelenting. The woman drives me insane. One minute, she wants me, then she ignores me. When I think she's finally coming back around, she tells me to lose her number. Every time I turn around, this woman is swapping shit up on me.

We were supposed to be done with all this back and forth, and yet, not even three hours back in town, I'm being hit in the face with something else. If she wasn't so fucking enraging, I'd walk away. But somehow, she has burrowed under my skin, invaded my fucking soul, and she refuses to release me from her spell.

She tries to sweeten the kiss I'm assaulting her with, but I won't allow it. How can she piss me off and turn me on all at the same time? I break the kiss to yank her shorts and panties down right before slamming inside her. A strangled moan comes out of her, letting me know she felt more pain than pleasure, and the thought excites me.

Maybe now she knows how her lies make me feel. I come just by the thought alone, not caring that she's still on the edge, knowing I didn't even warm her up before using her body for my own pleasure. Slipping from her, I tuck my cock back into my jeans and zip them up.

When I step away from her, she rounds on me, eyes blazing. "What the fuck was that about?"

She's angry. Good. I'm fucking pissed too.

"What's wrong, Kitten? You don't recognize a revenge fuck when it fills your tight cunt?"

Her eyes widen a fraction before hardening. "So that's it? You storm in here and fuck me like some savage whore, and then what?"

"You tell me! I'm not the one who hatched this insane plan. What did you want? How long was this supposed to go on?" My voice is rising, the hurt turning to anger. I didn't realize how much I was hoping Kennady was lying until right this moment.

"Yes, I agreed to go to that bar and meet you. I even agreed to fuck you that first time, but I didn't keep fucking you for Kennady," she screams.

"Right. And I'm supposed to believe that." I take a breath, trying to calm down. "Kennady told me everything."

She scoffs, pulling her hair from the bun. It falls in soft waves down her back. "I'm sure she did. Just like she told me all about you." Her eyes run up and down my body, clearly not liking what she sees. "Mr. Unavailable. The man who went through women the way most men go through beers. Hit it and quit it, right?" With that, she walks down the hall and around a corner.

I follow closely, grabbing her arm and spinning

her to face me when she reaches the kitchen. "Is that what you think of me?"

"I didn't say that. I'm just relaying what was told to me." Her words are soft, almost too soft for my ears to hear.

"And you believed her," I whisper, running a hand down her arm.

She nods. "I did. And then I met you."

Dropping my hand, I step away from her. "Yeah, I remember perfectly how that night played out. And the weeks after. You believed her." It all makes so much sense now. How she was able to do what she did. When she believed I was with Lucy and didn't try to speak to me about it.

As if she can read my thoughts, she says, "Can you blame me? Everything I saw fit what she told me, not to mention the way you hurt her."

I spin back around, facing her. "Hurt her?" My eyes narrow in thought. "I've never even touched her. How the fuck did I hurt her?"

"What do you mean, you didn't touch her? You dated her."

"No the fuck we didn't. She's been chasing me for months. Then one night, she showed up and I was on a date. I ignored her all night, and finally, she fucking disappeared." I barely remember the night, only a feeling of gratefulness that I didn't have to see her anymore. It was exhausting.

"You never dated her? You didn't sleep with her?" Harriet asks, watching me.

"Fuck no. I know her type. My own mother was just like her."

"So it was all a lie?"

Taking her hands in mine, I pull her to me. "I don't know, Kitten. You tell me."

She tries to pull away, but I don't let her go. It's becoming alarmingly obvious that we were both lied to and set on this path of destruction. I can almost understand why Kennady would have a vendetta against me, but what the hell is her problem with Harriet? It just doesn't make sense.

"Is this what you think I wanted? Yes, I came to that bar the first night for her. But that's it. You think I wanted to keep seeing you? You think I would have kept fucking you for her?"

"I don't know what to think anymore. I can't seem to think at all around you. Everything I used to know no longer makes sense."

"How do you think I feel?"

"You infuriate me. I want to strangle you and then I want kiss you. I want to choke you senseless and then make love to you all night."

"Then do it," she says.

"Which one?"

"Both? All of them?"

Lifting my hand to her neck, I tighten my fingers around her throat and walk her backward toward the living room. Once there, I push her onto the couch. Her hands pull at the waist of my jeans, tugging them down my legs. Once they hit the floor, I step out of them, and still holding her throat, I shove her backward. Nestling between her thighs, I slide inside her.

"You like that, Kitten?"

"I'd like it more if you'd stop talking and fuck me," she says, rolling her hips and tossing us on the floor. I land on my back, my hands wrapping around her body as we fall. She lands on my dick. One minute, we're laughing and the next, her hips are circling, rising and falling with each swish.

I raise my hips, meeting her thrust for thrust until we're both panting and racing for the edge. My orgasm is building, my balls tightening once again. Slipping a hand between her thighs I circle her clit. She slides down my cock and grinds her pelvis into my hand. Her nails scrape down my chest as she leans forward, and then she is exploding around my cock. Her teeth bite into my shoulder hard, but she doesn't stop moving her hips until I'm pulsing inside her.

She falls on my chest in a heap of limbs and sweaty flesh. Wrapping my arms around her, I hold her close until our breaths even out once again. Slowly, she slides off my cock and stands, her tee falling to the tops of her thighs. I pull myself into a sitting position and glance up at her.

"Just so we're clear, that was for you, right?"

"Fuck you," she says, laughing and offering me a hand.

"I just want to make sure we're on the same page."

"It was always for me, Pacey. Every single time."

I can live with that. There may have been a hundred things competing to tear us apart, but somehow, we made it to this point. And there's nowhere else I'd rather be.

Ten
months
later

Pacey

epilogue

THE WEATHER IS UNSEASONABLY cool for an August day, but I'm not complaining one bit. Checking my phone one more time, I search the photo for any hints, any information that will tell me where to go. In the background is an old Texaco sign. I zoom in, my heart racing with the thrill of the hunt.

Swiping the photo away, I pull up a search app then scroll through the possible locations until I find the place I need to go. Plugging in the address to my GPS, I head that way.

Twenty minutes later, I'm pulling in. Scanning the area, I search for any sign of Harriet but find nothing. Stepping out of the truck, I walk the area until I'm standing where I assume she stood to take the picture. Directly in front of me is another photo taped to an old wooden pole.

Snatching the picture, I scan it.

When I find her, I'm going to bend her over and spank her perfect ass for leading me on this wild goose chase. I mean, dinner and a movie would have been a lot less work. Ya know?

Luckily, this photo isn't too hard to figure out. It shows a trail through the trees about ten feet away. I hit the lock button on my key fob and make my way over to the trail. After about five minutes of walking, I come across another photo. This one is of Harriet standing in front of a giant oak, a shit-eating grin on her face.

Glancing down the path, I sigh and keep trudging through the woods. This pattern continues for at least thirty minutes. I walk for about five minutes and then find a new photo. The only thing that changes is Harriet's pose in the picture. In each one, she is wearing less and less clothing until I reach the end of the path. At the break in the trees is a single picture of Harriet lying naked on a swing. The same swing I see hanging from the front porch of a cabin across a small clearing about fifty yards away.

Shoving the pictures into my back pocket, I half walk, half run to the cabin. When I reach the door, I don't bother knocking. Pushing open the door, I step inside and call out her name, but only silence greets me.

Fucking hell.

Am I early? Did she not make it out here yet? I debate going back out to my truck, but then I see her car through a window in the kitchen. So, I know she's here . . . somewhere. Sliding my phone from my pocket, I call her cell as I walk through the cabin. When she doesn't answer, I call it again, but this time, I hold it away from my ear and listen for the ringing on her end.

There.

I can barely hear it, but it's here somewhere. Following the sound, I find myself back outside. Every time her phone goes to voicemail, I hang up and call again. It takes longer than I'd like to admit. Then she's there, lying across a blanket under the shade of a weeping willow in the back yard.

Her eyes light up when she sees me, a smile stretching across her face. "You could have just texted me the address, ya know."

"Where's the fun in that?" she says, standing. It's that moment, when the blanket falls to the ground, that I realize she is completely naked. Her nipples pebble from the cool air. I step forward, pulling her to me, and press my lips to hers. It's like coming home after a long time away. Her mouth fits against mine like her lips were created to match mine. My cock jumps to attention as her body molds to mine.

Breaking away from her mouth, I slide my arm behind the curve of her ass and scoop her into my arms before squatting down and laying her on the makeshift bed. Staring down at her, she looks how I would imagine a mythical fairy creature would look. Ethereal and beautiful. Her hair streams out around her like a golden crown, her skin flushed with fall's first kiss.

Kneeling beside her, I trail my fingers down her chest, across her abdomen, and between her legs. When I press inside her, her back arches. Leaning forward, I pull a nipple into my mouth, dragging my teeth along the puckered edge.

"Oh, Saints." She moans, weaving her fingers into my hair.

Curling my fingers, I pump into her while rubbing the base of my palm across her clit with each push inward. Her breath is coming out in pants, and after spending the last ten months teasing orgasms out of her, I know she's close to coming. Pulling my mouth from her breast, I settle between her thighs.

I drag my tongue along her crease and around

my fingers still buried deep inside her until she's coming unglued, arching her back off the mattress. Her breath hitches, and then her pussy is clenching around my fingers as her orgasm shatters in waves through her. I let her ride the waves as I gently coax each tremor from her body until she's digging her hand into my hair and pulling me up, up, up.

Her fingers wrap around my cock, her legs around my waist as she guides my shaft inside her soaking wet core. I move her hand and push all the way in with single thrust.

Once seated inside her, I pause and slowly work my cock back out, determined to savor this moment. I want to take my time and worship every inch of her. Unfortunately, she has a different plan. Gripping my ass with her nails, she pulls my hips forward, filling her once again.

Deciding there will be time enough for a thorough lovemaking later, I give her exactly what she craves. Wrapping my hands around her hips, I lift her off the ground and pound into her. Each punishing thrust brings us both closer to the edge.

Reaching between her legs, I rub a calloused pad across her clit as my balls tighten with the need to fill her. Then my orgasm is rushing through me. Harriet's legs tighten around my waist, her fingers digging into my arms as she follows me over the edge.

Completely spent, I collapse beside her and pull her into my arms before pressing a kiss to the side of her head. "Well, that was fun."

Harriet sits up and faces me. "It was, wasn't it? But unless you want to share all this" —she waves a hand down her body— "with the guys, we should get dressed."

"The guys?"

"Yeah. Everyone will be here soon."

"Everyone? Here?"

She sighs in exasperation. "Yes. Lucy mentioned how you all meet up once a year to camp, and while I love the idea, I'm not much for bugs and bears. So, I invited everyone here this year."

"You mean to tell me I have to share this cabin with Ash, Carson, and Weston? And here I planned to fuck you on every surface imaginable all weekend."

She tilts her head, considering. "Hmm. I suppose we could make them set up tents in the yard instead."

I grin, standing to pull my jeans back on. "That's my girl. Come on, let's go lock all the doors before they get here."

We gather up everything, and as we're headed back inside, gravel crunches. I glance down at Harriet, who is staring back up at me wide-eyed. Without missing a beat, we both yell, "Run!" and take off laughing.

Racing inside, I slam the door shut behind us as Asher reaches the steps. Gasping for air, Harriet twists the locks and leans against the door. Withing minutes, the pounding ensues. "I suppose we could let them stay for the weekend."

"But should we?" I ask, pulling her into my arms and nuzzling her neck.

Giggling, she pulls away and unlocks the door. Asher is the first one in, followed closely by Carson, who punches my arm as he passes. Harriet leans over and presses a kiss to the spot he hit before standing on her tiptoes and whispering in my ear.

"I own the place. We'll kick them out Sunday and stay the rest of the week alone."

"I love you, Kitten."

"I love you, too. Now, let's go make sure no one takes the master bedroom. It has a big ass tub, and I fully plan to be fucked in it later tonight."

I follow her through the cabin, thankful for the millionth time that this little blonde bombshell fell into my life. Even if I never would have planned for it, having her in my life makes it complete. Pressing a hand to my pocket, I feel the ring still there where it has been the last two weeks, just waiting for the perfect moment to ask her to be mine.

Forever.

Something tells me this weekend will be life-changing. And I am here for it.

acknowlegments

IT'S THAT TIME AGAIN. Whew. Getting this book done and out took everything in me. But I couldn't have done it without a few very important people.

Ceranyse, thank you for being as excited about Pacey's story as I am and for calming me down when I was freaking out about people Harriet. You rock.

Riley, thank you for always being willing to plot with me. Even if we get majorly off course and forget what we were talking about.

Carley, thank you for always being willing to read my second, third and fourth drafts. Oh and for sexting with me. It helped. Lol

Anna, who has been so amazing. I hope you love Pacey as much as you did Weston.

To my readers, who have supported this dream of mine. I couldn't do this without you. I know it has been a whirlwind the last few months, but I am truly so thankful for you all.

about sutton snow

SUTTON SNOW IS a labor of love for me. and a dear friend. We have been weighing options for a while now, unsure if we should create a new pen name for the spicier books or publish everything under the our personal accounts.

In the end, we both decided to make something unique together.

If you are new here, and aren't aware, HI! My name is Tinley Blake. I will be writing under Sutton Snow along with a friend of mine (who is choosing to not be listed for now) for all our darker, spicier novels. I hope you have a look around and find something you like.

Visit her website to find out more:

Suttonsnow.com
Join her Facebook reader group:
Smutty Suttys
To contact Sutton, please email her at
author@suttonsnow.com

about tinley blake

TINLEY BLAKE HAS SLEPT under the stars in Las Vegas, eaten dinner at midnight with French men who couldn't be trusted to keep their mouths on their food, and traveled across the countryside in stolen vehicles with worldwide drug men and lived to tell the tale.

She likes stories about family, loyalty, and extraordinary characters who struggle with basic human emotions while dealing with bigger than life problems. Tinley loves creating heroes who make you swoon, heroines who make you jealous, and the perfect Happily Ever After endings.

These days, you can find her writing in a sweet bungalow on the outskirts of Birmingham, Alabama, with her very own French man who is now her loving husband, their four kids, two dogs, and one very confused cat named Goat.

Visit her website to find out more:
Tinleyblake.com
Join her Facebook reader group:
Tinley Blake's Readers
To contact Tinley, please email her at
author@tinleyblake.com

also by tinley

SECOND CHANCE ROMANCE
THE WAY WE LOVED
THE WAY WE FOUGHT

ENEMIES TO LOVERS
LIAR LIAR: VOLUME ONE

ROMANTIC COMEDY
SEXPLORATION

SPICY BOOKS
UNBROKEN
UNBOUND

DISTORTED TRUTHS & PRETTY LIES

about sutton snow

SPICY BOOKS
UNBROKEN

UNBOUND

DISTORTED truths & PRETTY lies

TINLEY BLAKE

DISTORTED TRUTH & PRETTY LIES

Blurb

THERE ARE two things you should know about Nolan Pierce. One, she is the only daughter of William Pierce, the most powerful lawyer on the East Coast. And two...she's a liar.

Nolan is tired of pretending to be the perfect daughter. The truth is, she was never very good at being good. She loves breaking the rules—living on the edge of danger.

But she just bit off more than she can chew. And not even dear ole dad can save her now.

There are two things you need to know about Kaius King. One, he's the head of a criminal empire. And two...he gets what he wants. No matter the cost.

Kaius is intrigued by the rumor of a southern belle using his name, and by extension his power, to gain credibility. Even more so when he learns it's his lawyer's daughter.

But what starts out as a simple game of cat and mouse quickly becomes much more. And this time, his prey has one thing he doesn't... nothing to lose.

As Kaius and Nolan collide, it's a battle of wills the East Coast hasn't seen before. Only time will tell if their union will end in salvation or ruin.

PROLOGUE
NOLAN

I MURDERED MY FATHER TODAY.

The thought should terrify me, should make my heart ache and my stomach roll, and it does. But I'm also relieved to not be forced to lead two lives anymore. There is no longer a need to lie. I'll no longer be required to plan out every possible conversation down to a T. He knows exactly who his 'sweet baby girl' is now.

The absolute, soul-shattering relief of no longer having to hide who I am from the man who created me and gave me life eclipses any fear and shame I carry.

It also put him in the hospital.

I turn, peering through the thick glass into his

room. There are lines everywhere, running to his chest and hand, to the oxygen mask taped to his face, and the IV going straight into his arm. The monitor beeps regularly, tracking his pulse rate, monitoring his heart. I tuck my hands into the pockets of my denim jacket to keep from wringing them and end up digging my nails into my palms instead. The sharp, stinging pain grounds me in a way only pain can.

Time passes without measure as I stand there staring into his room, watching for any sign of movement. The mirrored image in the glass is my only companion. But she's no friend. Her eyes reflect the cold, hard, ugly truth.

I did this.

I killed him.

Me.

My eyes travel the length of his body. He seems so small here. It's hard to connect this image with the picture of him that's stored in my mind. Growing up, he was always larger than life. Everyone seemed to know him, no matter where we went. And they all respected him. He was kind and loving. I can count on one hand the number of times he raised his voice at me. Even those few times, it wasn't out of anger but rather disappointment. I tried my best to be the girl he needed me to be, even if it was all a lie, a façade designed to ensure I disappointed him.

My gaze reaches his face, and my eyes connect with his. Open. His eyes are open, and he is staring straight back at me. My breath catches. I take a step forward, and then another. His eyes widen. The monitor next to his bed jumps, the lines across it rising, rising, rising, and then stopping. A single line streams across the screen. A flatline.

All hell breaks loose. Nurses storm into the room, a flurry of activity. They lay him flat on his back, move wires, attach new ones. Someone grabs paddles and presses them to his chest. I turn away as a single tear escapes, leaving a salty trail down my cheek.

I did this.

My father. My mentor. My protector. He gave me the world on a silver platter, and all he ever asked in return was that I follow his one rule. One simple request.

I've never much liked rules. Unless, of course, I was breaking them.

CHAPTER ONE
NOLAN

SPEEDING through the streets with one hand on the wheel, I fumble through my purse in search of the ringing cell. Of all the times for my phone to not connect automatically to the car, it would be when I'm running late. The light changes from glowing green to stark red in a flash. I hit the brakes, tires locking up. My steering wheel shakes with the effort, but I stop just across the white line and take a deep, settling breath before answering the call.

"Hey, Dad, I'm almost there."

"Okay, dear. I'll go ahead and grab our table. Water?"

"Yes, thank you," I say, hanging up just as the light changes back to green.

Parking is tight when I pull up to Bakers, but I manage to squeeze my coupe in without hitting anyone. When I step through the door, the hostess greets me with a nod. She doesn't bother asking my name. My dad and I have been coming here for years, always on the second Thursday of the month, and we always sit at the same table. To be honest, they probably have our food prepared before we even arrive. Grilled chicken salad for me and three-cheese lasagna for Dad.

He's sitting there now. When he sees me enter, he stands and opens his arms. I step into them, breathing in his familiar scent and fighting back the urge to cling to him. After the last few days I've had, I could stay in his embrace. Safe. But that would lead to questions I don't have the answers to, so I pull back, paste a smile to my face, and sit across from him.

"How's school?" He takes a sip of his sweet tea and then places the glass back on the table.

"Good. Stressful, but good." It's always the same questions followed by the same answers. Every week.

How is school?

Good.

How is work?

Great.

It's a routine I crave, especially right now. Every other aspect of my life is slowly falling apart around me. I need this—a quiet moment suspended in time just for us. No distractions. No interruptions.

Our food arrives all too quickly, and I'm placing the napkin in my lap when dad's cell phone rings. He glances at it on the table, worry etching into his features. It's obvious he needs to take the call, but we decided long ago to not let anyone or anything interrupt our standing date. He presses the button on the side, silencing the tone, but it continues vibrating against the wooden tabletop.

"You can take it if you need to," I tell him.

He sighs and stands. "I'll be just a second, dear. Promise."

I nod and pick up my fork. Dad steps away from the table but doesn't go far. I can still hear his side of the conversation.

"Yes, I understand. Of course. I'll be right there," he says, running a hand through his short clean-cut hair.

With great effort, I hide my shock and dismay at the thought of cutting this short. We always take this time away from our busy lives to show up for each other. Whoever was on that call must have immense pull if Dad plans to go now. He places the phone back on the table, but not before I see the name across the screen. Four innocent letters connect to form a name I both hope to never hear nor see again. Dad opens his mouth to apologize, but I cut him off.

"Let's have lunch boxed up. We can finish at the office," I offer, preventing him from having to explain.

His shoulders slump in relief.

If only he knew.

I'd hoped to sneak in a few sly questions about King over lunch. It was a long shot, as getting Dad to give up any information on his clients was always tough. But this was better. If I played it right, I might get answers all on my own.

We walk back to his office since it's right across the street. The atmosphere when we enter is slicing. Everyone in the building is on edge, not a single voice raised above a whisper. My heart races in my chest with every step closer to Dad's office.

"Pierce." His voice cuts through me.

"King. Good to see you again," Dad says, taking King's hand in his own. "Have you met my daughter?"

Stepping through the door, I come face-to-face with the most glorious looking man I have ever seen before. He is all chiseled muscles and sharp

angles. This is King. The man who brings night-
mares to life. I smile, shoving my fears down deep.
King's gaze travels up my body as he steps closer.
By the time his eyes lock on mine, it feels as if I'm
standing here exposed, a chill licking my skin. It's
as if he's taking in everything about me and cata-
loging it all, from the way I stand to the placement
of my arms and my hands. His gaze tracks every
movement of my body, from the breath leaving my
lungs to the pass of my gaze over him.

"I don't think I've had the pleasure. Nolan, is
it? Nolan Pierce."

He knows. He knows everything. The walls
close in around me. Terror seizes my voice. I can't
get out of this. Somehow, he learned of me, and
he's here to tell my father. That's what was so
urgent. That's why my father abandoned our
lunch to rush here. When King demands your
presence, you appear.

I give myself two breaths to completely lose it
internally, and then I do what I do best. I fake it.

"Ah, so this is the King I've heard so much
about." I let my eyes travel up the length of him
the same way he did me, meeting his gaze head on,
and shrug. "I expected . . . more, I suppose."

My father freezes in place, glancing between us,
more than likely expecting King to slit my throat

right then and there, but he won't. I might not know him well, but I've always been good at reading people. The King likes a challenge. And I have just issued him one he won't be able to deny. It might be the only thing that saves me now.

He hides his shock better than most. I only see it because I'm looking for it. Then he grins, and any upper hand I thought I might have crumbles at the cold, calculating look in his eyes.

"This won't take long," King says, facing my father once again.

"Right. Of course," he stammers. "Nolan, would you mind?" Dad asks with a nod to the door.

I meet King's gaze one last time before stepping out and closing the door behind me.